If You Were MINE

ANNE SCHRAFF

URBAN UNDERGROUND®

SADDLEBACK
P U B L I S H I N G
www.sdlback.com

ISBN-13: 978-1-62250-041-3
ISBN-10: 1-62250-041-5
eBook: 978-1-61247-699-5

Printed in Guangzhou, China
NOR/0313/CA21300355

17 16 15 14 13   1 2 3 4 5

CHAPTER ONE

Pop! Pop! fourteen-year-old Chelsea Spain screamed, exploding through the front door like a gust of wind.

"Hey! Hey!" Pop responded, emerging from the kitchen. "What's hap'nin', little girl? The end o' the world here? All those doomsayers turn out to be right after all? The sky fallin' down? *What*?"

Pop was wearing an apron and a puffy white hat. He was cooking the family dinner, as he often did. Mom, Monica Spain, was too busy teaching fourth grade to cook, and that was okay with her family. When she did cook, her dinners came in plastic dishes out of a cardboard box, fresh from the freezer and microwave.

"We're gonna have a play at school!" Chelsea cried. "They said it's an original play, and it's just for freshmen to be in. But everybody can come and see it. This really great lady wrote it, Jeannie Duvall. Mr. Wingate, the drama teacher, is picking kids for the parts, and I'm trying out for the main role. I already talked to Mr. Wingate, and he likes me."

Chelsea stopped chattering to take a breath. "He said I got a lot of enthusiasm, and I got a real good chance. He said I was a 'live wire.' "

"Hey, that's great, little girl. You sure are a live wire there," Pop agreed, giving his daughter a bear hug. "Oh boy! Your brother did such a good job when he was in that play from *A Tale of Two Cities*. Now you're gonna be the family star. Way to go, little girl."

"It was so much fun seeing Jaris up on the stage when he was a junior," Chelsea recalled, her voice bubbling. "I thought, 'Oh, I could never do that.' But now I'm sure I can. The play is titled *Courage*, and it's about Harriet Tubman when she was just a young girl like us."

Both Chelsea and her brother, Jaris, were students at Harriet Tubman High School. "I'd get to play Harriet herself, Pop—I mean, if I get the part. And I honestly think I'd be better than anybody else in the whole freshman class."

"Absolutely," Pop replied. "Hey, a little over-the-top confidence isn't a bad idea at a time like this."

"You wouldn't believe," Chelsea grumbled, shaking her head. "That snarky little Kanika Brewster is trying out too. Like that mean old thing could play a wonderful, compassionate lady like Harriet!" Chelsea grimaced. "I mean, when she read for Mr. Wingate, we all had to cover our mouths to keep from laughing. She acted like Harriet was some little snob instead of a poor slave girl."

Mom came through the front door, and Chelsea swung her head around to look at her. Mom was dragging her heavy briefcase full of homework to be corrected. She dumped it on the floor and plopped down in one of the overstuffed chairs, kicking off her shoes.

"Mom! Mom!" Chelsea exclaimed. "I'm gonna get to play Harriet Tubman in a play at school—well, maybe anyway. We already had first readings, and I could tell Mr. Wingate likes me best. Some of the others were really awful. I was just telling Pop, this phony Kanika Brewster was the worst of all. We had to laugh."

Mom frowned. "Well, sweetie, it's rude to laugh at another person's efforts," she remarked.

"No, Monie," Pop declared. "I've seen this kid, this Kanika. She's this prissy little twit who thinks her family and her are better than everybody else. I don't blame the little girl and her friends for laughing. I remember when we had this parents' night a coupla weeks ago. Everybody is bringin' these nice homemade cookies. Well, in comes Kanika's snotty mom with these gourmet tarts from some highfalutin store. And you know she did that just to make everybody else feel crummy. Everybody grabbin' for the tarts, and the poor chocolate chip and raisin cookies the other moms baked got lost in the crumbs."

Chelsea was laughing hysterically.

"Next time we got one of these parents' nights," Pop announced, "I'm gonna spring something on her. I'm gonna make her tarts look chintzy. I ain't figured it out yet—maybe tiny little cream puffs or somethin' like that." Pop wore a devilish grin.

"Lorenzo," Mom groaned, "sometimes I think I have three children, Jaris, Chelsea, and you."

"Anyways," Chelsea went on, "Athena Edson is trying out too. But she wouldn't make a good Harriet 'cause she's just *too* pretty."

"*You* are very pretty too," Mom responded.

"Thanks, Mom," Chelsea said, "but I don't look like Athena. I mean, she's gorgeous, but

I'm just, you know, okay. Harriet Tubman was a really plain girl, and I could kinda play down the good stuff about me. People would believe me as Harriet, but Athena could come out in rags and still be beautiful."

"Athena Edson," Pop noted. "She looks like one of those dolls, the Barbie doll type. To tell the truth, the kid makes me sick. She looks like a twenty-year-old woman in a kid's body."

"And the other girls trying out, I don't even know them," Chelsea continued. "But one of them had this little squeaky voice, and nobody could hear what she was saying. I feel really good about my chances. Old Maurice Moore told me I was the best. He said if I win the part, he'll give me a kiss. I told him I'd smack him if he did that, and he just laughed. He likes to tease girls."

"Stay away from the little creep," Pop commanded.

"He's okay, Pop," Chelsea said. "He's kinda like the dog that's always yapping, but he never bites."

"I seen him looking at you, little girl," Pop commented. "When you're wearing your clothes too tight, y'know what I'm sayin'? Like you're pretending to be a sausage or something that got stuffed in the casing. I don't like how he looks at you."

Next to come through the door was Jaris Spain, home from Tubman High. Chelsea told him all about the play and how she thought she had a good shot at playing the lead. "Lemme give you a good tip, chili pepper," Jaris advised. "When they make the final decision, this Jeannie Duvall is gonna make you or break you. Mr. Wingate is sweet on this lady. So when you do the reading, you look right at her and do it for her. I did that when I was trying out for Sydney Carton in *A Tale of Two Cities*. I ignored Wingate and everybody else, and I just played to her."

"Okay! Thanks, Jaris," Chelsea said. "I just met the lady once. She's pretty. I could see that Mr. Wingate liked her."

"Any good parts in the play for boys?" Pop asked.

"Well, there's this boy Harriet helped to escape," Chelsea answered. "Then this horrible slave master got so mad he threw a lead weight at the boy. It hit poor Harriet in the head, and it made a dent in her head. She had bad headaches after that. The play sorta makes it look like Harriet and the boy were sweet on each other and stuff. But that's what Ms. Duvall does to make the story better, makes it sort of a love story."

Chelsea giggled. "Heston Crawford is trying out for the boy. So is Maurice. Another one trying out is a friend of Sharon's— Keone Lowe. He was pretty good."

"Keone Lowe," Jaris noted. "Isn't he the boy who saw Zendon kill that guy over on Grant?"

"Yeah," Chelsea said, "isn't that awful to see a murder happen? Keone was too scared to talk about it. Then the cops arrested Zendon on suspicion, and Keone came forward and told his story. I hope

I never see the stuff Sharon sees over on Grant. I think I'd have nightmares forever and ever."

"Keone a freshman at Tubman?" Pop asked, with a nod of his head.

"Yeah. He's real quiet," Chelsea answered. "He's Sharon's boyfriend, but I don't have any classes with him. You know how it is, Pop. The kids that come from the apartments on Grant, they don't mix with kids like Athena and Keisha and me. They hang with each other."

"Well, that's not entirely a bad thing," Mom commented. "Most of the people over on Grant, I wouldn't want you being close to anyway. Sharon is all right, but it's a tough, gang-infested neighborhood. Those people don't have the same values we do. I'm sure some of them are nice, and they can't help they live in the projects. But the kids have to be absorbing all that bad stuff that goes on there."

"Yeah," Pop said, rolling his eyes comically. "Don' wanna be hangin' with the losers, little girl. You gotta stick with the winners. Those poor folks in the projects, they got a disease—poverty. It's like the flu, you know. They get too close, and they'll sneeze on you, and pretty soon you're poor too. Gotta hang with people like Athena Edson. Her folks got money. No sense, but plenty of money."

Chelsea knew her father didn't mean a word he said. He was being sarcastic. Pop didn't believe in shunning people just because they lived on Grant Street.

Mom glared at Pop and then went on. "It's nice that you have friends whose parents are professional, quality people." She had listened closely to Pop's tirade, and she realized he was being critical of her comments.

"Especially that Athena," Pop went on, wagging his head and popping his eyes out even more than before. "Talk about quality professionals. Trudy Edson, she teaches high school to a bunch of poor kids. Athena's father, I ain't clear what he's out there doing. I think he's probably selling no-good life insurance policies to gullible people. Sure, Athena hangs out at the twenty-four-seven store half the night, swishing her little bod to get whistles from the passing punks. Man, if that ain't quality, I don't know what is. Get the thugs in their beaters to honk their horns at your cute little butt, and, man, you're talking top-o'-the-line quality."

"Lorenzo!" Mom finally announced. "You are being difficult again. You know perfectly well what I'm talking about. How many shootings have there been over on Grant? You know what kind of people live in those apartments. They don't work. They're taking money from the government. *Our* tax money, I might add. They're raising their children to be lazy and dishonest."

Jaris felt he had to chime in. "Trevor Jenkins is my best friend, and he comes from poverty, Mom. His mom had to raise her kids by herself because her husband was no good. Those four boys were

11

jammed in that little house. They ate oatmeal and beans and rice. You couldn't want better people than the Jenkinses. Two of the boys are in the army now, and they're doing well. And Kevin Walker. Look where he came from, and he's the best. He's got your back anytime you need a friend. And Derrick Shaw—"

"All right, Jaris," Mom interrupted, glaring at her son. This conversation always went down this way. Mom presented her logical and very reasonable views. Pop ridiculed her in his sarcastic way. And the kids, Jaris and Chelsea, chimed right in on Pop's side. They made Mom feel like an idiot or a snob, maybe both.

"I'm teaching kids from Grant in my fourth grade," Mom continued. "I know what I'm talking about. You don't even have to look at their home addresses to know who they are. They're the ones who come to school without their hair combed. They come in the same shirt three times a week, with the same egg yolk stains on the pockets. The parents just don't care. That's the way they are."

"Hey, I hear you, Monie," Pop said. He was standing in the kitchen door, waving his arms in the air. He looked comical in his white apron and puffy chef's hat. "Even teachin' those kids is a big waste of time." Pop slapped his hips. "I say don' even bother sendin' 'em to school. When they're done with day care, don't march them off to kindergarten. Just send them straight to prison. Gonna end up there anyway. Kiddie prison. They could paint cartoon characters on the walls so the little crooks wouldn't feel so bad. Maybe Mickey Mouse and those guys from *Sesame Street* in little striped jail jumpers."

Mom pushed up from her chair. "Why do I bother discussing anything with you people? You just demean me and make a fool of me. So I may as well get at this mountain of homework."

After Mom left the room, Pop winked at Jaris and Chelsea. "I'm makin' picante pork chili tonight, you guys. Green bell peppers, tomato, and salsa, tender pork ground up. Mmmm! Your mama gonna forget all about her stuck-up ideas when she starts getting a whiff o' all that." Pop grinned and returned to the kitchen.

Chelsea plopped into the chair Mom had been sitting in. She was quiet for a few seconds. "Know what, Jaris?" she remarked. "Sharon … I like her a lot, but she's not as … clean as my other friends. Her hair sorta … smells. I guess she doesn't wash it every day. It bothers me. It shouldn't bother me. I don't want to be, you know, like looking down on her."

"Tell her in a nice way about washing it more, chili pepper," Jaris suggested. "When you go too long between washing your hair it smells like … hair. Some kids just don't get taught stuff like that from their moms."

"Yeah," Chelsea agreed. "I could like pretend my hair smelled funny. I could say, 'Oh darn, if I don't wash it every day, it smells weird.' "

"There you go, chili pepper," Jaris responded. "Sometimes that's all it takes. And another thing. You could have a nice shampoo in your purse, and you could pretend you don't like the scent. Maybe she'd like it 'cause you're just gonna toss it. Could be there's not enough money floating around for shampoo at Sharon's house."

"That's a *great* idea, Jare!" Chelsea bubbled. "I'll do that tomorrow. You know what? You're not half bad as a big brother, Jaris." Chelsea jumped up and headed for her room. She wanted to text all her friends about the play.

That night, Jaris was working at the Chicken Shack. He had worked there since he was a sophomore. They served fried and grilled chicken legs, wings, and nuggets, along with sandwiches and salads. Jaris's boss, Neal Wendt, liked him. Now Jaris had been promoted to assistant manager, and one of his new duties was to hire people.

"Some kids coming in this afternoon, Jaris, about the counter job," Neal reminded him. "They've turned in their applications. You need to sit down with them and do a short interview. We got three coming in, so you pick the best of the lot."

Neal was in his middle thirties, and he was a nice guy. Jaris didn't want to let him down. But Jaris was uncomfortable about deciding who got the job and who'd be turned down. Only a couple of years ago, Jaris had been a nervous applicant, sitting at one of those tables and being interviewed. He had really wanted the job. Jobs were harder to come by now, even harder than they were then. Jaris figured all three of those kids would be hoping against hope they'd get the nod.

Later in his shift, Neal said to Jaris, "They're here." Jaris was making chicken sandwiches at the time. He glanced over the display case to see two boys and a girl. They all looked about sixteen. They all would probably do a decent job if he hired them. But Jaris could pick only one.

Jaris finished the sandwiches and went out into the customer seating area. There, he told the trio he would interview them one by one. He went to a nearby booth and sat down. While waiting for the first applicant, he thought maybe one of these kids needed the job badly. Maybe there were economic problems at home. Or maybe they just wanted more spending money. But Jaris couldn't let thoughts like that figure in his decision. He had to be fair to the Chicken Shack and Neal. He had to pick the kid he thought would do the best job.

Fortunately, none of the three were students at Tubman High. Two went to Lincoln High, and the third attended a private school nearby.

"So," Jaris asked a thin-faced young man with glasses, "do you think you'd like working here?"

"Oh yeah," the kid replied. "I worked the ice cream concession at the county

IF YOU WERE MINE

fair, and I enjoyed that. I'm real good with people."

"It says here on your application that you go to a private school," Jaris noted. "How's that working out for you?"

"Real good," the boy, Mason Scott, answered. "Better teacher-to-student ratio. I'm not a real great student, and I would kinda be lost in the shuffle at public high school."

Jaris then posed the questions he'd decided to ask. Mason replied positively, and Jaris thought he was a good candidate.

The next boy, Lonnie Hoover, was a muscular guy from Lincoln High.

"You're a wrestler, huh?" Jaris remarked.

"Yeah," Lonnie responded, "it's a great sport for building your body and your confidence. The girls all come to watch too, and that's cool." Lonnie grinned.

"I bet," Jaris said, smiling. He liked this guy. He had more personality than Mason, and personality was valuable in a restaurant. The customers liked friendly kids.

Sometimes the older customers came in just to banter with kids about the same ages as their grandchildren.

The rest of the interview went well.

The last applicant was Amberlynn Parson. From a distance she looked pretty. Close up in the booth opposite Jaris, she was stunning. She had gentle fawn eyes and a lovely oval face. Her lips were very full. Jaris got goose bumps just looking at her. He was grateful that his girlfriend, Sereeta Prince, wasn't nearby to see the stupid expression on his face.

Jaris spoke in as businesslike a voice as he could muster. "I see from your application that you worked at a hamburger place last summer, Amberlynn." Jaris was just a bit older than these kids. He felt ill qualified to be judging them, but that was the job. "How did you like it?"

"Oh, I loved it," Amberlynn replied with enthusiasm. "The people were all so nice and so grateful when you gave them a smile and, you know, a little extra service. I guess they don't expect that in a lot of places. I tried to make each customer feel like their satisfaction was really important."

Her answer didn't surprise Jaris. Amberlynn had given her former employer's phone number as a reference. Jaris called it and spoke with the manager there. The manager had nothing but good things to say about her.

"That's good," Jaris agreed. "Did you sell anything besides hamburgers?"

"Oh yes, all kinds of drinks, salads," the girl answered. "I looked at the menu you have here, and it was about the same at the hamburger store." Amberlynn seemed really smart. She handled the rest of Jaris's questions well.

With the interviews over, Jaris retreated to the kitchen. He thought they couldn't go wrong in hiring any of the three. They seemed like good, serious kids. "It's tough to pick one," Jaris told Neal.

"Welcome to management, boy," Neal laughed. "So, which one?"

Jaris looked out at the three. After a long sigh, he said, "Amberlynn Parson."

Neal looked through the kitchen door at the girl, then back at Jaris. Jaris knew what Neal was thinking.

"Okay," was all Neal said with a shrug, and he went outside.

CHAPTER TWO

Jaris hoped he had made his decision for the right reasons. He wanted to believe that Amberlynn Parson was the best choice for the Chicken Shack. He didn't want to think that her hot looks might have dimmed his judgment.

Jaris could hear the girl's delighted squeal when Neal told her she had been hired. Jaris didn't look out into the customer area to see the two disappointed boys leaving. He kept telling himself he had made the right decision for the right reasons. Amberlynn was intelligent and outgoing. She seemed sincerely dedicated to serving customers. She was a perfect fit for the Chicken Shack. Besides, Neal had more guys working here now than girls. Balancing that out was good.

Still, Jaris felt troubled. A small inner voice taunted him, accusing him of hiring Amberlynn because she was so gorgeous. He had been determined to put everything but the best interests of his employer aside. But he had ended up acting like a guy, charmed by a pretty chick.

Trevor Jenkins was coming in to do his shift as Amberlynn was leaving. "Whoa!" Trevor gasped. "Did you get a load of that beautiful chick just leaving here? Man, she's so hot, my eyeballs are scorched!"

"She's the new hire," Jaris responded calmly. "Her name is Amberlynn Parson. She's a junior at Lincoln."

Trevor laughed. "Old Neal, he's got an eye for the babes! I bet it like took him a split second to hire her. I pity any other poor sucka who was applying for the job."

"I'm assistant manager now, dude. You know that," Jaris reminded his friend. "So I had to interview three kids, and I picked her."

23

Trevor was silent for a moment. Then he clapped Jaris on the shoulder. In a low voice, he said, "Good job, dude! She's the best eye candy I seen in a long time."

"I hired her because she seemed best for the job," Jaris insisted. "She's smart and enthusiastic. The two guys were good too. Fine school records, nice manners. But she was real friendly and customer oriented. It was a hard call."

"I bet it was," Trevor said, winking and smiling like a fool. Jaris liked Trevor. He was the closest thing to a brother Jaris ever had. They had been close since they were toddlers. But right now Jaris felt like wiping the grin off Trevor's face with a knockout punch.

"Man, I'm serious!" Jaris snapped. "I wish I could have hired all three. But we got mostly guys working here now, and we need a mix."

"You said it, man," Trevor agreed, still smiling foolishly. "I mean, like, man, you don't have to convince me. You made the right choice. I think you did a great job

24

hiring the chick. I bet business'll go up. Guys'll come in just to get a look at her."

"Well, I hope she's good," Jaris grumbled. "It'll be the first time I ever had a say in hiring somebody. I hope she works out."

"If she's as good a worker as she looks," Trevor commented, "she'll be the best thing the Chicken Shack ever saw." He paused then, and the smile faded. "You gonna tell Sereeta you hired her if the two of you come in here to eat?"

Jaris felt angry. He didn't know why he felt so angry, but he did. "Man, what are you driving at?" he growled at Trevor. "I should be ashamed of hiring a pretty girl to work here because Sereeta might get jealous? Is that what you're sayin', dude? Well, I got news for you. You got us all wrong, Sereeta and me. We have no doubts about each other. We're solid. If Sereeta and I come in here, sure I'll tell her I hired Amberlynn. I'll tell her why too, and Sereeta, she'll understand. She won't have any problems with it, okay?"

"Don't get steamed, dude," Trevor backed off. "I didn't mean anything."

"Sure you did," Jaris snapped. "You think I'm some jerk who hired a girl just 'cause she's pretty. Now I gotta hide it from my girlfriend. Well, you're dead wrong, Trevor. I hired Amberlynn because I think she's best for the job. Period. And get that idiotic smile off your face, man, before I hit you with a platter."

The shift that night was tense. Jaris kept second-guessing his decision. Trevor had not helped matters. Trevor was a good guy. He didn't mean to stir up Jaris's self-doubts, but he'd done just that. Jaris was often unsure of himself anyway. Like Pop, he was always questioning himself. He feared that the girl's looks *had* influenced him, and that thought bothered him.

Amberlynn Parson was scheduled to start work the next evening. Jaris wanted her to be great. He wanted her to wow the customers. He wanted Neal to see what a good choice she was. But another part of Jaris hoped she wouldn't show up. That would be a relief to him. Then he would call Lonnie Hoover, the wrestler from Lincoln.

After school the next day, Jaris stopped off at Spain's Auto Care to see his father. Pop (Lorenzo Spain) was an auto mechanic. He'd worked for someone else—old Jackson—for years. He'd felt like a failure, just a grease monkey doing another man's bidding. Now he owned his own garage: Spain's Auto Care.

To buy the place from Jackson, Pop had to put a big mortgage on the house. He had had a hard time convincing Mom to go along with that. But so far things were working out. Pop was making more money than Jackson ever made. Now that Pop was in charge, more and more customers were coming in.

"Hey, Pop," Jaris greeted, walking over to his father in his crisp mechanic's uniform. Pop was leaning into an engine.

"Hey, Jaris," Pop replied. "You don't usually come by to visit. Somethin' on your mind, boy?"

"Yeah, you got ten minutes?" Jaris asked.

"Sure. We'll grab some sodas and talk," Pop said. "I was gonna take a break anyway." Pop yelled over to his young assistant, Darnell, "Hey, Darnell, I'm about finished here. Will you wind it up? The lady comin' for her beater any minute now."

"Sure, Mr. Spain," Darnell responded.

Pop laughed. "I keep tellin' the kid to call me Lorenzo. But he's old school even if he is a kid. I like that." Pop and Jaris went into the office with their sodas and sat down at the desk. When Jackson owned the garage, the office was dirty and messy, and the chairs for the customers were ragged. Now everything looked clean and sharp.

"Pop, I told you I'm assistant manager down at the Chicken Shack," Jaris began.

"Yeah, that's great," Pop acknowledged, popping the tab on his soda can.

"Pop, I had to hire a new kid," Jaris went on. "I hated it. Three of them came in, two guys and a chick, and they all looked good. I agonized over it, and then I ended up hiring the girl. I thought she was smart and friendly and she'd be good for business. We're kinda top-heavy now with guys. But Pop … she's really hot. I'm thinking now that maybe that played a part in my decision. Now I feel bad. I mean, just looking at her gave me goose bumps, and I'm ashamed of myself for being a jerk—"

"Hey, Jaris, you're a guy," Pop counseled. "Any guy doesn't notice a hot chick is ready to be put in the ground, y'hear what I'm sayin'? Hot chicks come in here to have their beaters fixed. You better believe I do a double-take on 'em, especially if they're dressed skimpy like chicks are these days. But it don't mean anything, Jaris. I don't change the way I fix their beaters. I don't charge them less. And I know you, boy. You hired that girl 'cause you thought she'd do the best job. That's the only reason you hired her." Pop took a long gulp of the cold soda.

"Pop," Jaris moaned, "I sat there like an idiot, staring at her. It was like I never saw a cute chick before. Sereeta's the most beautiful girl on earth, and I love her with all my heart. What's with me?" Misery pooled like dark water in his mind.

"Jaris, I love your mom more than I love myself," Pop advised. "If I had to, I'd die in her place without even hesitatin'. She's my life. I wouldn't want to be on this earth without her bein' with me. But I notice the pretty women who come by. It don't mean nothin', Jaris." Pop drained the last of the soda from the can and tossed it into the recycle container.

"This chick you hired," Pop continued, "if she messes up, you'll fire her. I guarantee you that. If she works out, you'll be glad you made a good business decision. Besides, you won't even notice her pretty soon. She won't be any more to you than the hot sauce on the chicken wings. Trust me, boy. You're beatin' yourself up for nothin'. Don't be beatin' yourself up, boy. The world's gonna do enough o' that without you doin' it to yourself." Pop leaned across the desk and squeezed Jaris's shoulder.

Jaris smiled. "Thanks, Pop. I feel better," he said.

"Anytime, kid," Pop declared, laughing. "It takes one to know one."

Jaris headed home. He had a lot of work to do on his AP American History class for Ms. McDowell. She'd been trying desperately to rescue her brother, Shane Burgess, from the street gangs and drugs. But he was now in police custody for drug possession. Yet she would be in class tomorrow, as demanding and inspiring as usual, helping her students do their best. She swallowed her own worry and pain in order to devote herself to her students. Jaris admired her for that. Ms. McDowell had inspired Jaris, and he admired his mom's work as a teacher. He was now pretty sure he would be a teacher too.

Jaris finished his work for AP American History and then headed for work at the Chicken Shack. Trevor Jenkins wouldn't be there tonight, and that was okay with Jaris. He was sick of Trevor teasing him about hiring Amberlynn. Trevor was just joking, but it was a sore spot with Jaris.

Amberlynn showed up for her first shift earlier than scheduled. That was a good sign. She got into her yellow and white Chicken Shack shirt and looked even cuter.

"Hi, Jaris," she said in her sweet voice. "I'm a little nervous."

"You'll do fine," Jaris assured her. "You just work with me and watch what I'm doing. When you get comfortable, take over. I'll be right here to help you out."

All evening, Amberlynn was at Jaris's side, her large, lovely eyes taking in everything. Jaris could tell she was smart. She was a fast learner. Midway through the shift, Jaris stepped back and let her begin taking orders. She was good. She didn't get things mixed up. If the customers wanted grilled chicken, they got it. If they wanted vinaigrette dressing on their salad, they got it.

Jaris was pleased. He felt happier with his decision to hire her. She was smart, friendly, and efficient. That's what counts in working with the public. No matter how cute or handsome the servers are, if they mess up orders, they hurt business. Jaris remembered a young guy Neal hired who mixed up most of the orders. One angry woman threw her sandwich at him. The poor guy was fired that night.

Jaris noticed something else too. A lot of young guys were coming in, including some of his friends. They'd been tipped off about the hot new chick.

Oliver Randall and Matson Malloy came in—without their girlfriends. "Hey," Oliver told Amberlynn, "you're cute enough to be on TV, girl."

Amberlynn smiled politely and replied, "Thank you. Do you want ranch or vinai-grette for your salad?"

Matson Malloy's eyes were popping out of his head. Jaris thought it was a good thing Sami Archer, his girlfriend, wasn't with him. But, Jaris reminded himself, Pop had explained things well. Noticing a hot chick doesn't mean you want to dump your girlfriend. It just means you're a healthy guy.

A little later, Kevin Walker came in with Carissa Polson, his girl. They'd had a rocky time when Carissa briefly dated another guy, but everything was cool now. Kevin ordered two chicken sandwiches and salads. Carissa looked at Amberlynn and asked, "Where do you go to high school?"

"Lincoln. I'm a junior at Lincoln," Amberlynn answered. "You guys from Tubman?"

"Yeah," Kevin replied. "We're gonna beat your socks off at the next track meet."

Amberlynn was perfect in her response. "Well, may the best team win. What kind of dressing on your salad?"

When Kevin collected their takeout order, he spoke quietly to Jaris. "She's hot. She lights up the whole place, man."

Carissa laughed and grabbed Kevin's arm. "Come on, Romeo, she's probably got sixteen boyfriends."

Kevin laughed, and they left with their order.

Still later, Marko Lane and his girlfriend, Jasmine Benson, came in. Jasmine took one look at Amberlynn and gave Marko his instructions. "Just sit down here, boy. I'll get our order. I know what you want. No need for both of us standing in line."

Jasmine gave her order to Jaris, but she kept staring at Amberlynn.

"Girl, you a model or something?" Jasmine asked.

Amberlynn shook her head. "Oh no. I'm just a junior at Lincoln High School," she answered.

Within minutes, the order was ready. Jasmine grabbed the tray and hurried back to Marko. She saw him craning his neck for a better look at Amberlynn.

"Look at that babe, Jaz," Marko remarked. "She hardly looks real. Looks like some doll come to life or something."

"Come on," Jasmine commanded. "Let's not eat in here. It's too crowded.

IF YOU WERE MINE

Let's get bags and take our stuff to the car. It's a nice cool night. We could stop at the outdoor patio down the street."

"Who's she?" Marko asked.

"Like I know," Jasmine snarled. "Come on, fool, take your bag. Let's get out of here."

Marko followed Jasmine obediently out of the Chicken Shack. When she wasn't looking, he took one more quick glance back at Amberlynn.

Business tapered off around nine thirty. The Chicken Shack closed at ten on week-nights. After ten, there weren't enough customers to justify staying open.

"Well, how'd I do?" Amberlynn asked Jaris and Neal.

"You did great, Amberlynn," Neal responded. "Efficient, nice. My assistant manager here, Jaris, he did well to have hired you. I don't remember when we last had a new hire as good as you."

"Yeah, you were impressive," Jaris agreed.

"Thanks, guys," Amberlynn said, exhaling a big sigh of relief.

36

"So, Amberlynn," Neal asked, "how did you get here, and how are you getting home?"

"Oh, no problem," she replied. "I live right on the bus line. The bus stop is right down at the corner. I'm home in twenty minutes."

Neal lived a quarter block from the Chicken Shack. He walked to and from the store. The other employee, Paul, got picked up by his girlfriend. Many times Jaris walked or jogged home, but tonight his Honda was parked outside.

"Uh, Amberlynn, you planning on waiting at the bus stop in the dark?" Jaris asked.

"It's fine," Amberlynn assured him. "The bus is due in about ten minutes. I'll be fine. I told my mom I'll be home around ten thirty."

Jaris sighed deeply. He wasn't ready to offer her a ride. It was the last thing he wanted to do. But at night, the streets filled up with gangbangers and dangerous guys looking for vulnerable people. A few weeks ago, just a stone's throw from the store, a guy was murdered over a drug deal. And a month ago, not far from the Chicken Shack, some dudes tried to force a woman into their car. Only her screams saved her. No woman—much less one as pretty as Amberlynn—had any business waiting at a dark bus stop.

"I can drive you home," Jaris offered.

"Oh no, I don't want to put you out, Jaris," Amberlynn protested. "It's sweet of you to offer, but I'm perfectly okay taking the bus. Honest."

"Well, I'm not okay with it," Jaris responded. "Look, Amberlynn, for most night shifts, there's another girl here, and she lives over your way. Jenny's very nice, and maybe we can work something out. But tonight I better drive you home. It's not a problem. I'd just worry about you standing there in the dark."

"Jaris," Amberlynn objected, "you're so sweet. But I feel like I'm imposing on you—"

"Come on," Jaris commanded. "My Honda's parked outside."

"Won't I make you late going home?" she asked.

"No, it's fine," Jaris insisted, leading the way to his car. He was thinking how little he liked doing this.

Amberlynn got into the passenger side, and Jaris glanced over at her. "Buckle up," he told her. Shc had the sweetest profile. Marko was right. She looked like a doll. She smiled and buckled up. She was so hot, even the seat belt looked good on her.

CHAPTER THREE

On the highway, Jaris would have headed south to go home, which is where he wanted to be. Instead, Amberlynn told him to go north. She said she lived on Woodland Lane. Jaris had never heard of the place. Once off the highway exit ramp, he looked eagerly for the street sign.

"It's a mobile home park," Amberlynn explained. "It's about another mile. Just past a gas station."

"Okay," Jaris nodded. He didn't know why he was so nervous with Amberlynn in the car. Being nervous was stupid, and yet he was. He stared ahead anxiously, looking for the gas station that would mean they were almost there.

A full moon hung in the sky, and near it, the planet Venus shone like a bright jewel. Years ago, Jaris's mother had pointed out that sometimes the moon and Venus are close like that.

"We're almost there," Amberlynn noted. "That's the gas station." Then she asked, "How long have you been working at the Chicken Shack, Jaris?"

"I started when I was about a sophomore," Jaris answered. He was relieved to have something to talk about. "I just mopped up around there. And I helped unload the truck when it brought supplies. I was real part time. But then, when I got to be a junior at Tubman, they hired me as a regular employee. It's been a good deal for me. I've saved some money and got some good experience too. I was able to buy this car with what I've saved working there. It's an old beater, but it gets me where I want to go. I don't ask much more than that from a car."

"Now you're assistant manager. Wow," Amberlynn remarked.

IF YOU WERE MINE

Jaris was peering into the darkness, wanting Woodland Lane to show up real fast. "You seem to really know what you're doing around the Chicken Shack," Amberlynn went on.

"I should after all this time," Jaris responded.

"I bet you got all kinds of plans for college after you graduate high school," the girl said with obvious admiration in her voice. "You seem like the kind of a guy who's got it all together."

Jaris didn't like where the conversation was going.

"No, usually I don't have it together at all," he objected pointedly. "But I got some ideas. My dad wanted to go to college, but he got a sports injury and lost his athletic scholarship. His big dreams didn't happen for him. He's spent a lotta years regretting that. I'm sure I'll go to college. Community college, then State. I'll have to work, but that's okay."

"There's the driveway into the mobile home park." Amberlynn pointed. "By the palm trees." Jaris saw a weather-beaten sign for Woodland Lane—at last.

Jaris turned the car into the lane. Amberlynn poked a finger at one of the homes. "Right there, the green one. I live there."

Jaris had been taking notice of the mobile home park. It was small. Maybe forty or fifty homes in all were lined up on narrow streets. Jaris thought it must be weird to live in one of these parks where you had hardly any yard. You could reach out your window and almost touch the neighbor's house. But Jaris had once been inside a mobile home. Inside, they looked like regular houses except that the ceilings were low. For tall people like Jaris, it was a little unnerving.

He parked in front of the pale green mobile home. There was a little planter in front, filled with pink and white geraniums. Amberlynn got out of the car and turned to say, "Thanks so much for the ride, Jaris. And thanks for hiring me. I didn't think I'd get the job. I thought one of those guys would get it. I need the job very much, so … well, thanks."

"Well, you got off to a great start tonight," Jaris told her.

After a second or so, Amberlynn spoke softly. "My father lost his job, and he's having a hard time finding another one. So my paycheck is really going to come in handy."

"That's good," Jaris responded. "I gave you the schedule for your shifts, right?"

He'd worked out her schedule with her for after classes at Lincoln and on the weekends.

"Yes, I have it right here," Amberlynn replied. "Night."

"Good night, Amberlynn," Jaris nodded.

Jaris watched her walk to the door of the green mobile home, unlock it, and go in.

Inside the mobile home, Amberlynn Parson put three chicken sandwiches and three sodas on the kitchen table.

"They sell us these for half price 'cause we work there," Amberlynn explained.

"It's a good deal. They're really good sandwiches. We get other perks working at the Chicken Shack too. When buns get too old and stuff, they give them to the employees." She smiled at her parents. She was proud that she was bringing not only money home, but added perks as well.

She and her parents sat down to eat.

"How did the first night go, honey?" Mom asked. "I know that every beginning is hard. You were probably real nervous—"

"Oh, Mom, it was good," Amberlynn interrupted. "It was much better than I expected. I worked right alongside this assistant manager, Jaris, the guy who hired me. He's such a good teacher, calm and patient. He kinda slowed down what he usually does so I could see how it's all done. He's a senior at Tubman High, but he's so mature. He seems much older. When I got to take orders myself, he stood there right with me to cover for any mistakes. But I didn't make many."

The girl took a sip of her diet soda and then went on.

"He smiled and said I was a real fast learner. Like, we've got to ask customers how many creams they want with their coffee and stuff. They used to keep the creams in a bowl of ice cubes on the counter, Jaris said. But people were coming in and just taking hand-fuls. I feel really good about tonight."

"I got a couple more weeks on my un-employment checks," Amberlynn's father commented. "Today I was down there at the employment place. They posted some new jobs. I applied for two of them. I think things'll be turning around in the construc-tion business pretty quick. Then there won't be so much pressure on you, honey."

Amberlynn nodded. "Yeah, I think so too, Dad." She smiled at her father. He wasn't young anymore, he was almost fifty. He and his wife had four children. But they were all up and gone, except for Amber-lynn, the baby.

"Are they nice down there, Amber-lynn?" Mom asked. "Sometimes in these fast-food places they can be mean."

"Oh, Mom, Neal, the boss, he's nice and funny," Amberlynn replied, gulping a bite of her sandwich. "But Jaris, oh my gosh! He's so nice and so handsome. I mean he's tall, and he has these dark, dreamy eyes. He's like mysterious-looking and kinda gloomy. Then this smile breaks out on his face, and it's just amazing. He gives me chills! My heart was pounding so hard when he was standing next to me. I tried to be cool, and I don't think he noticed, but I was like swooning!"

"He probably has a girlfriend, honey," Dad advised. "Or maybe several."

"I don't know," Amberlynn smiled and rolled her eyes. "He didn't say anything about a girlfriend. I got the feeling he liked me. He wants to go to college and be a teacher. I dated some boys at Lincoln, and they were okay. But this Jaris, he just puts them all in the shade!"

Amberlynn had been so happy she got the job and could help out at home. But now she was happy for another reason too.

She had just met the most attractive guy she had ever seen.

"He wouldn't let me wait at the bus stop 'cause he was worried it was dangerous, so he drove me home! Can you imagine?" Amberlynn cried.

"I guess maybe he *does* like you, honey," Mom replied with a grin and a quick glance at her husband.

Jaris drove home thinking about the girl. He felt better now about picking her for the job. She needed the job. Her father was unemployed. They didn't seem to be a very prosperous family to be living in a mobile home park. Jaris felt sorry for her. She was a kid with her first decent job, and she probably wouldn't be keeping much of her wages. Jaris was lucky that way. His parents always did okay. He could keep his salary for stuff he wanted and even start a little bank account.

Then, as Jaris drove down the dark highway, he noticed something. A car ahead of him was moving very slowly. At first he thought the driver was just being very cautious, perhaps nervous driving at night. Maybe it was a very elderly person unaccustomed to night driving. But then the car began drifting over the yellow centerline and back again.

Jaris began to think that the driver might be drunk. The on-ramp to the freeway was coming up in a couple miles. A drunk driver could get on the freeway and cause a horrible accident. Jaris pulled out his cell phone, wondering whether he should alert the highway patrol to this suspicious driver.

Then Jaris recognized the car. He'd seen it often in the teachers' parking lot at Tubman. It belonged to Jaris's English teacher, Mr. Langston Myers.

Jaris sped up and pulled alongside the car, honking his horn. He motioned to the driver to pull over, pointing to the shoulder of the road. The driver was Mr. Myers all right. He was traveling at about fifteen miles an hour, and he looked startled to see Jaris trying to communicate with him.

Mr. Myers turned onto the shoulder of the road and stopped the car. Jaris pulled his Honda in ahead of him. Jaris got out of his car quickly and went to the driver's side of the car.

"Hi, Mr. Myers," Jaris said. "Are you okay?"

"Of course, I'm okay," Mr. Myers replied in a slurred voice. "What on earth did you flag me over for? What's going on? If you needed to speak with me, you could have done so during school hours, you know."

"Mr. Myers," Jaris began slowly, "you were going really slow, and the car was drifting. I thought maybe you were sick or something." Jaris smelled the alcohol on the man's breath.

"I'm fine," Mr. Myers declared. "There's nothing wrong with me. I'm on my way home. Now, if you do not mind, get out of my way, Mr. Spain."

Mr. Myers looked bleary-eyed. Jaris suggested, "Mr. Myers, I would be glad to drive you home if you're not feeling good."

"I beg your pardon," Mr. Myers protested indignantly. "The audacity of a teenager insinuating that I am unfit to drive. I have just been to a book signing party and—"

"Please, Mr. Myers," Jaris pleaded. "Let me drive you home. I don't want you or anybody else getting hurt. I'll park my own car right here. Later on, my friends'll drive me back to pick it up."

Mr. Myers stepped from the car. He almost fell down, but he caught himself on the door. He was even drunker than Jaris suspected. He shook his finger in Jaris's face. "I know what you are thinking, you impudent young fool," the man sputtered. Spittle sprayed from his mouth as he spoke. "You think I am in-tox-icated. Well, I have never been more sober. I shall reenter my car now and drive home. I command you not to interfere."

"Mr. Myers," Jaris asserted, "I don't want to call the cops. But I will if you try to drive off."

"How dare you threaten me?" Mr. Myers shouted. "You witless young idiot." Then the man realized that he could be facing police officers and the humiliation of a sobriety test. He could even be arrested for a DUI. That thought calmed the teacher down a bit. He fumbled for his cell phone and soon was talking to his wife. "Diane, a very upsetting thing has just happened. I was about to get onto the freeway on the way home from the book signing party. Then some obnoxious young twit forced me onto the shoulder of Highway 16. The wretch is accusing me of drunk driving. He said he'll call the police. You and Les please come at once. Then Les can drive your car home."

Mr. Myers then fell silent. Someone was speaking to him.

"Of course not," the man objected. "I'm not drunk. But I did have a drink at the party. If this impertinent boy does call the police, I could be very embarrassed."

Off the phone, Mr. Myers glared at Jaris. "You have humiliated me for no good reason. Just wait until my wife and son get here. They will give you a piece of their minds that you shall not soon forget! The outrage of what you have done!"

Mr. Myers stumbled to the passenger side of his car, steadying himself on the car with one hand. He bumped his head getting in and didn't seem to notice. He nearly fell into the seat and then righted himself.

"Oh brother, what a night!" Jaris thought. He looked at the disheveled man. One of his drinks from the cocktail party stained his white shirt. "I'm sorry, Mr. Myers," Jaris mumbled.

"Be ready for the tongue-lashing of your life, you impertinent do-gooder," Mr. Myers warned. Jaris thought he was now probably doomed in English. Mr. Myers would hate him forever because of what Jaris did this night. But what else could he do?

Presently, a white sports car pulled onto the shoulder behind them. The driver was an attractive woman of about forty. Sitting beside her was a heavyset, college-age youth, undoubtedly the son, Les.

"Ah!" Mr. Myers gurgled with an evil grin. "Now you will hear from someone who knows me well. She will tell you that I have never driven under the influence of alcohol!"

Diane Myers was not smiling as she and her son got out of her car. She glanced quickly at Jaris, who was leaning on the driver's side of the car. "Are you one of his students?" she asked in a strained voice.

Jaris pushed off the side of the car. Somehow he felt as though he shouldn't seem too relaxed—which he wasn't. Besides, he wasn't sure how Les was going to react to the goings-on.

"Yes, ma'am," Jaris replied. "I saw him driving funny. I was afraid he'd go on the freeway, you know, and have an accident."

"I am sorry you have been put to all this needless trouble, Diane!" Mr. Myers's trumpeting emerged from his car. "But this wretched boy—this hoodlum—"

54

Mrs. Myers leaned into the driver's side window. "*Stop it!*" she hissed through clenched teeth.

Mr. Myers fell silent in midsentence. He stared out the windshield, looking confused. The son looked disgusted. "Can I go now?" the son grumbled. "Gimme your keys, Mom."

Diane gave her son the keys to her car, and he quickly took off. Then the woman turned to Jaris.

"I am very sorry," she apologized, "that you had to be involved in this. If the police had discovered him in this condition, it would have been disastrous. I hope what happened here tonight doesn't become common knowledge. My husband is a good man. He doesn't deserve to have his career trashed by gossip—"

"Mrs. Myers," Jaris interrupted, "I won't mention this to anybody. I swear that to you. I won't even tell my mom and dad. As far as I'm concerned, tonight never happened. Okay? Mr. Myers is a good teacher.

I enjoy being in his class. He made a bad mistake tonight."

"Thank you," Mrs. Myers responded in an emotional voice. "Thank you very much … *for everything*."

Jaris watched the couple drive off in their car with Diane Myers at the wheel.

Then he got back into his car and continued his trip home.

When Jaris got home, his mother was still working on the computer. "Jaris, you're so late," she noted. "I was getting worried. Everything okay?"

"Oh yeah, Mom," Jaris assured her. "That new hire at the Chicken Shack. She was gonna take the bus home, but it was dark. She'd have to wait at the stop. It worried me, so I drove her home. You never know who's roaming around at night."

"That was nice of you, Jaris," Mom commented. "I'm about done here. I'm beat. I'm going to bed."

Jaris wanted to tell Mom about the other reason he was late. But he had promised

Mrs. Myers that he would never mention what happened on Highway 16. He swore he wouldn't tell anybody, and he would keep that promise. Whenever Jaris gave his word, he felt duty-bound to honor his promise. Jaris hated gossip anyway. He just hoped that, when Mr. Myers sobered up, he would forgive Jaris for what he had to do. Jaris was counting on an A in English. He'd feel really bad if this incident cut his chances. Surely, he thought, Mr. Myers had to realize that driving drunk was wrong. Jaris could have just called in an anonymous tip to the police without getting involved. But doing that would have gotten the teacher in major trouble. Jaris chose a course that was more dangerous to himself, and he hoped Mr. Myers would appreciate that.

Langston Myers was a good English teacher, but he aspired to be a published writer. He had written a novel set in the days of the Harlem Renaissance in the 1920s, when black music and literature flourished in New York. But no regular publisher would print the book. So Mr. Myers turned to a subsidy press: he paid to get his book printed. The man then made the mistake of telling everyone, in high spirits, that a regular publisher was putting out his book. He lied.

But Marko Lane found out about the real story and spread it all over Tubman High. Marko had been having trouble in Mr. Myers's English class, and this was his way of getting back at the teacher. Marko wanted to humiliate him by telling everybody the book wasn't good enough to interest a regular publisher. Poor, pathetic Mr. Myers had to pay to have it printed.

Jaris suspected that Mr. Myers's humiliation had started him drinking. Jaris doubted the man was coming from a book-signing party tonight. He was probably coming from a bar.

Jaris remembered the hard times before Pop bought the garage from old

Jackson. Pop's spirits were low. He was nearing forty, and he felt like a failure. He was just a grease monkey working for somebody else. He'd often stop at a bar on the way home. When he did, the whole family would worry about his condition as his pickup came into the driveway. How close had he come to having an accident? Or did he have a DUI? Jaris loved and respected his father. It broke his heart when he saw Pop down on himself and drinking too much.

Now Pop had sworn off drinking completely. The proud owner of Spain's Auto Care, he was like a new man. That gave Jaris so much joy.

Jaris felt sorry for Mr. Myers too. The teacher had done a wrong and stupid thing, but he had been brought low. He had been so happy to share the excitement of his newly published book. Then Marko Lane had turned his joy into humiliation.

Jaris felt nervous going to English class the next day. He was determined to act as though nothing had happened. He would force himself to ask interesting questions. And he would look rapt and attentive when Mr. Myers answered them. When his gaze met Mr. Myers's eyes, Jaris was going to try to show that he still liked and respected his teacher. Jaris would try to show that nothing had changed.

But what would Mr. Myers be thinking? Jaris dreaded coming to class and facing his teacher. But how much more did Mr. Myers probably dread coming to class and seeing the kid who stopped him for drunk driving?

Jaris knew that stopping Mr. Myers's car was gutsy and maybe foolhardy. But he couldn't let an obviously impaired driver get onto the freeway or even keep going down Highway 16. Jaris had to do something. He didn't want to hear on TV later that the Myers's car had caused a bad accident and maybe deaths. Calling 911 would have been the safest way to go. But Jaris knew that he would hurt Mr. Myers badly if he did that. So he would have called 911 only if all else had failed.

Jaris walked slowly into English. He glanced back at Marko Lane, sitting in his usual place, a smirk on his lips. Marko was ranting to Jasmine about Mr. Myers's book.

"I bet it's pure garbage," he sneered. "Otherwise, a regular publisher woulda taken it."

"Shhh!" Jasmine snapped. "I think he's comin'. You wanna get us both in trouble?"

CHAPTER FOUR

The door opened. Jaris stared at the floor for a minute. He dreaded seeing Mr. Myers. But he couldn't postpone this moment forever. He looked up, prepared to smile if Mr. Myers looked in his direction.

But Mr. Myers wasn't entering the classroom. Instead, Mr. Pippin was dragging his battered briefcase. He was substituting for Mr. Myers. He looked older and more defeated than when he taught them junior English last semester. "I am filling in for Mr. Myers," he announced in a dull monotone. "It will be just for today."

With a sigh, Mr. Pippin dropped his briefcase on the desk.

CHAPTER FOUR

"Mr. Myers said you are studying great poetry," the teacher began. Then he seemed to have another thought.

"For heaven's sake, you are almost adults," he pleaded. "You are seniors. Let's have a civilized class. Let's behave as if we were worthy of the free public education you are receiving at the expense of the poor taxpayers." As he spoke, he looked directly at Marko Lanc. He looked half in supplication, hoping that somehow Marko had become a more decent, kinder person. But his gaze also held hatred because he knew that that could not be so.

Marko sat bolt upright in his chair. "Oh, Mr. Pippin!" he cried out in an enthusiastic voice. "Is it ever good to see you! I wish you were taking over this class permanently. I mean, I know I wasn't always the best student in your class last year. But now I appreciate all you did. This guy who teaches this class, this Mr. Myers, he's no good. He's got these delusions that he's a writer and stuff. You know what went on there—"

"Stop!" Mr. Pippin commanded. "Stop at once, Marko Lane. Mr. Myers is an excellent teacher. I will not have you defaming him. He is a friend of mine and a man I deeply admire."

Stopping a moment while still glaring at Marko, Mr. Pippin seemed to be composing himself. "Now," he continued, "will somebody tell me what you have been studying in poetry?"

"See," Marko persisted, "that's just it, Mr. Pippin." Jasmine nudged Marko to be quiet, but he ignored her. "He doesn't give us real poetry that, you know, has stood the test of time like you used to do."

Mr. Pippin leaned on his desk. It all flooded back to him. It was last semester. It was *déjà vu*. Junior English all over again.

Marko Lane raved on. He couldn't be stopped. Like a wild beast that has spotted vulnerable prey, he barged ahead. "He's been giving us this junk, Myers has, this black poetry, you know, in dialect. Like you know, 'little brown baby wif spa'klin' eyes.' It's insulting to have to hear stuff like that, like we're morons or something."

Oliver Randall cut in. "Mr. Pippin, Mr. Myers spent like two minutes of the last dozen class periods on dialect poetry like that. Paul Dunbar wrote a lot of poems, and they're worth studying. But Marko is acting like that's all we do in here, and that's not true."

"Good, thank you," Mr. Pippin responded gratefully. He recalled Oliver from last year. He thought Oliver was a breath of fresh air. "So, I see you've been studying William Butler Yeats. So let's focus on his 'A Prayer for my Daughter.' "

"Is he sick or what?" Marko asked.

"Is *who* sick?" Mr. Pippin demanded, rage disfiguring his face.

"Old Myers," Marko replied. "Why isn't he here? Not that we want him or anything, but what happened to him?"

"You do not refer to your teacher as 'old Myers,'" Mr. Pippin sputtered. "Have you no respect for anybody or *anything*? If you refer to him at all, which I prefer you did not, you refer to him as 'Mr. Myers.' As for why he is not teaching this class this morning, it is none of your business."

Mr. Pippin shook his head in frustration and disgust. He riveted his gaze on Marko. "Have you read the poem?" the teacher asked.

"Uh, yeah," Marko answered. "This old dude in the poem is worried that his daughter's gonna be too beautiful. He thinks she's, you know, not gonna be kind and stuff. He's thinking a kind, ugly girl is better than a mean, pretty girl." Then the old Marko kicked in. "But that's kinda stupid 'cause no guy is gonna bother with some ugly chick if she's kind or not."

Mr. Pippin stared longingly at the clock on the wall. He looked as though he wanted to will the hands to move faster. He only wanted that blessed moment when he could escape this classroom.

Sereeta spoke up. "Mr. Myers told us that the poet, Yeats, had gone with this really beautiful girl named Maud. But the girl was so busy fighting for Irish independence against the British that she didn't have time for Yeats. A lot of his poetry was really personal."

"Yes," Mr. Pippin responded, brightening. "Did another of Yeats's poems even more powerfully express his unhappiness with women, based on his personal experiences?"

Oliver raised his hand. "Yeah. 'No Second Troy' was the poem where Yeats comes right out and says it. The girl filled his life with misery because she was promoting revolutions."

"He didn't get fired, did he?" Marko Lane asked out of the blue.

"*What*?" Mr. Pippin demanded.

"Mr. Myers." Marko replied. "I thought maybe they fired him 'cause he lied about getting his book published. He's not that good a teacher anyway … and then bragging about it like he did. That wasn't very cool. I don't see why you can't teach this class regularly, Mr. Pippin. You weren't that great last year, but you're way better than Mr. Myers. That's for sure. I bet most of us in this class would be glad to settle for you, Mr. Pippin. Especially after having Myers for a few weeks."

Mr. Pippin told the students to open their books and look at some of the other poems by William Butler Yeats. He asked them to find a favorite and, in no more than one hundred words, to describe why they feel that poem was effective. Then Mr. Pippin sat down heavily. For a moment, he pressed his fingers into his closed eyes, and his shoulders hunched over more than usual. Occasionally he looked up at the clock, closely watching the progress of the hands. When the longed-for moment came, he roused himself to a standing position. Collecting the student papers, he grabbed his old briefcase and fled like a victim escaping the scene of a crime.

Outside the class, the students gathered to gab about the absence of Mr. Myers. "He seemed okay yesterday," Oliver remarked.

"He's really embarrassed that every-body knows he lied about his book," Marko announced.

"He didn't lie, Marko," Oliver objected. "He never told us who the publisher was."

"Yeah, but everybody thought it was a real publisher," Marko insisted. "He let us think that. Then when he got caught, he was all embarrassed and everything."

"That was really crummy of you to spread that all over the school, Lane," Kevin Walker told Marko. "You need to go to the doctor and have your heart exam-ined. Maybe he could tell you why it is not working, dude."

Jaris could only imagine what Marko and his friends would do with the story if they knew what had happened last night on Highway 16. Of course, they would never know. Jaris would never talk about it.

Jaris wondered whether Mr. Myers was not in class because he had a bad hang-over or was just unable to face Jaris. No doubt his wife had told him that Jaris had promised to keep the whole incident private. But did Mr. Myers believe her? Or did he think that right now the whole class was buzzing about him?

Jaris tried to sort out how Mr. Myers might be thinking. Would Mr. Myers really think that Jaris was regaling his classmates with all the juicy details? Would the teacher think Jaris was making himself a big hero? Mr. Myers had called Jaris an idiot and a hoodlum. If so, how could he be trusted to keep this secret? The temptation to share the story—and get back at the teacher—might be irresistible.

Mr. Myers probably thought Jaris had entertained all his friends with the story. Jaris could make himself look big and bold and important. After all, he forced Mr. Myers to the shoulder of the road, demanding a call for help because he was unfit to drive. What a funny story that could be. The tipsy teacher almost tumbles from the car, his shirt stained with booze, making threats and burbling in his slurred voice. So the story would go. And all who heard it would tell their friends. It could even go viral on the Internet.

In the end, when Mr. Myers returned to Tubman High, he would be a laughing-stock. He imagined walking back to the classroom to the knowing smirks and titters of his students.

"There he goes," they would say to one another, if only with their looks. "There's the drunk. Lucky that Jaris stopped him before he wrecked his car and killed innocent people. What a disgrace. How can a teacher act like that?"

Surely, Mr. Myers must be thinking the story had reached Marko Lane. In that monstrous boy's hands, the story was a weapon, used endlessly to bludgeon Mr. Myers.

"No wonder he didn't show up today," Jaris thought with sadness.

After school, Jaris planned to drive Chelsea home. She normally walked or biked home on her own. But today were the final tryouts for the play about Harriet Tubman, and Chelsea would be late. Jaris figured he and Chelsea would go for frozen yogurt when she came out. He could hear all about how things went at the audition. Jaris didn't want Chelsea to have to live through this special moment alone. As he waited for his sister, he sat in his car doing homework.

Chelsea came toward the car with a big grin on her face.

"How'd it come out, chili pepper?" Jaris asked her as she got in and buckled up.

"I'm not absolutely sure I got the part, Jaris, but I think I did," Chelsea answered happily. "We won't know for sure until Friday afternoon. But Mr. Wingate and Ms. Duvall were smiling at me. I think I really got into Harriet Tubman's personality. I feel good about it. Athena is sure she didn't make it, and Kanika was awful."

"Okay, it's off to the Ice House for a preliminary celebration," Jaris announced. He started up his Honda and drove out of the parking lot.

"Yesss!" Chelsea squealed. "And another good thing. Heston Crawford was very good as the boy Harriet rescued. You know, we had to dress like Harriet and the other slaves. So I wore this old faded dress and these big old shoes. And Heston, he wore this torn shirt. It was almost like he didn't have a shirt on at all, it was so raggedy. Wow, Heston's been working out, Jaris, and he looks so good. He used to be skinny but no more. He's been lifting weights and stuff. He's so ripped, Jaris. I got goose bumps just looking at him."

"Uh-oh," Jaris grunted, "not good."

"What do you mean 'not good'?" Chelsea asked. "I'm fourteen years old, and pretty soon I'll be fifteen. *Fifteen*!"

"Chronologically, chili pepper, this may be true," Jaris explained. "But to Pop's way of thinking, you're nine going on ten, and ripped boys don't interest you much."

"Anyways," Chelsea persisted, "when we were in science class, before Ms. Colbert showed up, Heston told me he liked me a lot. He said it'd be so great if we got to play together in *Courage*. It'd be so fun rehearsing together and stuff. Heston said I was pretty too. He's never said that before."

"Oh boy!" Jaris groaned. "Trouble on the horizon." He pulled into a parking spot in front of the Ice House.

"Jaris," Chelsea said as they walked to the door, "you told me you liked Sereeta already in middle school. You said you'd sit there in eighth grade and think how pretty she was. That's what you told me."

"Well, chili pepper," Jaris tried to explain, "this is a whole different thing. Dads don't worry if their boys are looking the girls over. Dads worry about their little girls, see. It's one thing if your son is checking out some young girl in eighth grade. But it's a whole 'nother deal if your little girl is the one some stud is eyeballing. See what I mean?"

Chelsea didn't reply. They approached the counter and put in their orders.

"I want a strawberry yogurt with real strawberries on the top," Chelsea said. Then she spoke to Jaris. "Heston is real shy. I think Pop likes him."

Jaris ordered a caramel yogurt with nuts. "So far he likes him," he admitted.

The following day, Jaris had lunch under the eucalyptus trees with his friends, as usual. He and his friends were the gang everyone called "Alonee's posse." Alonee Lennox had brought them all together. Jaris had been searching his mind for a way to tell everybody about Amberlynn. He didn't want Trevor or somebody else to bring her up. So Jaris unwrapped his liverwurst sandwich and lay back on the grass. After taking a bite, he said, "This new girl we hired at the Chicken Shack, she's really good. Her name's Amberlynn, and I broke her in the other night. She's really smart."

"She's hot too," Trevor remarked, grinning. Trevor was dating a girl named Shay since he broke up with Vanessa Allen.

Trevor had barely missed getting involved in a crime when Vanessa and her friends burglarized a house. Trevor liked Shay, but it wasn't going anywhere with her.

"Man," he announced to the posse, "I'm itching to ask Amberlynn out. I mean, right before we close, maybe I will. You think, Jaris? Or would she just laugh in my face?"

"I don't know," Jaris answered, "but give it a shot. You're scheduled to work the same shift with Amberlynn tonight. So go for it. I don't think she'd laugh in your face. She's too nice to do that."

"She that beautiful," Sami Archer commented, "she probably stuck-up, Trevor. Don't get your hopes too high, boy."

"Yeah," Trevor agreed. "You're right, Sami."

"But maybe not," Sereeta offered. "You're pretty cute, Trevor. You might be just what she's looking for."

Trevor grinned at Sereeta. "Thanks for the vote of confidence, Sereeta," he said.

"You're assistant manager down there. Huh, Jaris?" Oliver asked. "Did you hire her?"

"Well, I interviewed three kids, and they were all good," Jaris explained. "I hated to have to pick one. But she seemed so friendly, and she kept talking about how important it was to please the customers. She had experience at a hamburger place and a great reference. She seemed smart too."

Jaris didn't look over at Serceta. He just hoped she was okay with all this. "We've had some people working at the Chicken Shack that aren't too good with the customers," Jaris went on. "It's like somebody orders grilled, and they get fried. Then the kid just shrugs it off. Amberlynn wouldn't do that."

"I gotta stop by the Chicken Shack and see this girl," Alonee announced.

"Yeah," Sami declared, "me too. When Matson talked about her, he kept grinning in a real weird way. She seem like one hot chick."

Sereeta laughed and lay on the grass beside Jaris. She stretched, and Jaris turned to look at her. He thought she was so beautiful that it was hard to take his eyes off her. She wore a red-striped tank top and skinny jeans, and she looked perfect. Jaris reached around her shoulders and gave her a hug. "Love ya, babe," he told her.

"Love you back," Sereeta responded.

After lunch, Jaris headed for English class with even more dread. He felt really sorry for Mr. Myers. Once or twice, he thought about calling him. Maybe Jaris could assure him that nobody at school knew anything about the incident on Highway 16. He could make it clear that no one ever would. But Jaris was afraid to do that for fear of humiliating the man even more. Mr. Myers might think, "This schoolboy's assuring me that my sins are still secret, all thanks to him."

Jaris walked into English class with Sereeta. Today, English was after lunch.

"Jaris, you seem awfully nervous about this class today," Sereeta remarked. "Is something wrong?"

"Uh, no," Jaris replied. "I was just wondering whether Mr. Myers was going to be here."

"He probably had some business to take care of yesterday," Sereeta suggested, "something to do with his book. Do you know something that the rest of us don't know? Is he sick or something?"

"Oh no!" Jaris answered quickly. "It's just that he was kinda depressed after Marko taunted him about the subsidy publisher."

Jaris found it hard to picture Marko Lane as an adult. Marko was, like Jaris, almost seventeen. He'd be in college in a year. Then he'd be working somewhere. Jaris couldn't imagine him curbing his trash-talking mouth and being mature. Would he stand around the water cooler at his job, gossiping about the other employees? Would he ridicule the weird little guy in the next cubicle? Would someday a mob of angry coworkers lock him in the broom closet?

Langston Myers appeared outside the door, carrying his fine leather briefcase.

IF YOU WERE MINE

Jaris had never seen the teacher pause at the door and look into the classroom before entering. Mr. Myers glanced nervously at Marko. He seemed to expect Marko to be grinning from ear to ear, his mockery now fueled by what happened on Highway 16. Mr. Myers came in slowly. He seemed to be steeled against the whispers, snickers, and funny looks that he expected. He cleared his throat. He coughed. He took a quick look at Jaris, then looked away.

Jaris raised his hand immediately. "Mr. Myers, I read the chapter on musical devices in poetry, and I got it somewhat. But could you explain it in more detail? I'm kinda confused." He looked intently at Mr. Myers.

Langston Myers stared back at Jaris for a long moment. Jaris could sense the change in the man's demeanor. The teacher had come into the classroom expecting his shame to be common knowledge. He wore fear and embarrassment on his face. He felt he would not be respected anymore as the teacher in this classroom. He would be the drunk who

80

had to be stopped from going on the crowded freeway that fateful night. And he would be stopped by none other than an alert teen-ager from his own class. Mr. Myers had felt naked before his enemies. And, in Langston Myers's eyes, they were all his enemies.

But now Jaris was just a student again. He was eager to learn from his teacher, whom he obviously respected. He wanted help with a concept he couldn't quite grasp. The event on Highway 16, the car on the shoulder of the road, the angry words, all faded until they ceased to exist. The right order of things had been reestablished. In that moment, Mr. Myers knew that Jaris Spain told no one and never would. In his heart, Mr. Myers was both surprised and deeply grateful. But he would never say anything to Jaris, not a word. Nor did Jaris expect or want any talk about the matter. It was gone, like dust in the wind.

"Yes," Mr. Myers finally responded, "thank you, Jaris. ... That is, for bring-ing up that question. I think many of you are confused on the issue, and we need to discuss it. The musical element of poetry is often what makes poetry so enjoyable." Mr. Myers was speaking in his booming baritone voice. It was one of the best classes Jaris could remember.

After school, Jaris was glad he didn't have to work at the Chicken Shack. He had a lot of homework. He also didn't want to work alongside Amberlynn so soon. He had another day to think about his decision to hire her. He'd have his feelings sorted out. Tomorrow, it would be easier to work with her.

He and Chelsea were doing their homework in the living room when Pop came through the door.

"Oh, Pop!" Chelsea announced, looking up at her father. "They're gonna announce the cast for the Harriet Tubman play Friday afternoon. I'm so nervous. I'm pretty sure I got it, though."

"Hey, little girl, you got it nailed," Pop assured her.

"And I bet Heston Crawford is gonna be the boy she saved," Chelsea went on, "'cause he's got a nice strong voice."

Jaris kept his nose buried in his work, hoping Chelsea would leave it at that. But she didn't.

"And he really looks good in that torn white shirt he has to wear," Chelsea cooed. "He is so cut, Pop!"

Jaris pushed his nose a little closer to the laptop screen. Pop froze in place on his way to the shower. Then he turned and glared at his daughter.

"He's *what*?" Pop demanded. "He cut himself? Is that what you're sayin'?"

Chelsea giggled. Jaris tried to send mental messages to her—"Stop! Keep quiet! You're setting yourself up!" But Chelsea didn't read Jaris's mind.

"Uh, no," she giggled. "That's like really well muscled and stuff. He's such a stud and—" Chelsea finally realized she had gone too far.

"Well, ain't that nice?" Pop said, glowering. He was in his grease-stained overalls, standing in the middle of the living room. He folded his arms and put one hand to his chin. "Lemme get this straight. In this play, the actors, they don't like wearing clothes, right? I seen pictures of those awful slave days, little girl. And I don't see no guys walkin' around in the buff, y'hear what I'm sayin'?"

"No, no!" Chelsea responded quickly. "I mean his shirt is all worn and torn, but … he has his shirt on … "

"Oh, that's good," Pop said sarcastically. "Best to keep the shirt on. Best to keep *everything* on. This ain' no Vegas strip show, right? We're talkin' kids' doin' a play. We don't want no guys runnin' around like no jaybirds. So what's the teacher, Mr. Dingbat?"

"It's Wingate," Chelsea replied.

"Dingbat, Wingate, whatever!" Pop said with disgust. "I'm keeping an eye on this project, little girl."

CHAPTER FIVE

On Thursday afternoon, Jaris went to work at the Chicken Shack. Amberlynn was already there, wearing her yellow and white chicken shirt.

"Hi, Amberlynn," Jaris greeted. "How'd everything go yesterday?"

"Great," Amberlynn replied.

Jenny, the other girl at the Chicken Shack, chimed in. "Amberlynn's really good, Jaris." Jenny was twenty and married, and she had a baby. Her husband's hours at the machine shop had been cut, so she had to work part time. "Amberlynn and I worked it out. Whenever we got the same shift, she can ride home with me."

"Everybody's so nice around here," Amberlynn remarked. She tried hard not to stare at Jaris, but she wanted to. He was the cutest boy she had ever seen.

Business was slow in the early evening. Trevor Jenkins, alone, came in around eight. Jaris figured he was going to hit on Amberlynn if he hadn't done it last night. He was all dressed up in his Tubman track team jacket, and he looked good.

"Hey, Amberlynn," Trevor greeted. "How're the chicken tacos tonight?"

"Wonderful as ever," Amberlynn responded. "Salsa on the side?"

"Yeah, I love salsa. Always want extra," Trevor declared. He sat down at the counter, which was empty except for him. "I run on the track team at Tubman," he told her. "I'm pretty good. I have the second fastest time this year."

"Good for you," Amberlynn responded.

"You like track?" he asked her.

"It's fun to watch sometimes," Amberlynn said.

86

"You look so great," Trevor noted. "I bet you work out."

"Thanks, but I don't really," Amberlynn admitted. "I hate sweating and stuff. My brother used to wrestle at Lincoln. The sweat would be just pouring off him ... not for me."

"So, we got a meet against Lincoln coming up," Trevor commented. "You oughta come see it. Wednesday afternoon."

"Maybe," Amberlynn said, turning to another customer who had just come in.

Trevor could see that Amberlynn wasn't very interested in talking to him. Last night, when they shared the same shift, she acted the same way. Trevor was disappointed, but he wasn't going to give up. Tomorrow, when they would work together, he thought they could get to know each other better. Then maybe he could work up the courage to ask for a date.

Jaris kept an eye on Amberlynn, making sure she was doing everything right. New employees were not completely on their own for about a week. The assistant manager had to make constant checks.

Jaris was bringing a tray to a table when he heard a familiar voice. "Hi, Jaris," Sereeta called. She had come into the Chicken Shack with her mother, Olivia Manley. Mrs. Manley was a young-looking woman. She was wearing a blue and yellow T-shirt and cutoffs. She could have passed for Sereeta's older sister.

"Hi, Sereeta. Hi, Mrs. Manley," Jaris greeted. Amberlynn was busy, bringing coffee here and chicken sandwiches there. Sereeta looked at her and spoke to her mother. "Mom, Jaris just hired that girl. He's assistant manager here now. She seems to be a good worker."

"She's striking," Olivia Manley remarked. There was a faint look of envy in the woman's face. She herself was still a young, lovely woman. But whenever she saw a stunningly beautiful girl who was twenty years younger, she felt sad. No time in Mrs. Manley's life was as satisfying as

when she was a teenager. She was lovely
and fresh then, and the whole world was
opening for her like a flower. All dreams
and ambitions were possible then. There
were no "too lates" or bitter regrets. "Isn't
she striking, Sereeta?"

"Yeah, Mom," Sereeta agreed.

Jaris felt weird. Amberlynn had turned
out to be one of the most efficient people
who ever worked there. Neal even told him
that she was a gem.

Jaris thought, "Yeah, that's why I hired
her. She's a true people person. She can make
people feel special—the young, the old, the
in-between. She jokes with the customers,
but she never flirts." Yet his misgivings returned to him. How much did Amberlynn's
looks count when Jaris hired her?

Jaris lingered at the table where Sereeta
and her mother had sat down. "Sereeta, you
got anything going on tomorrow night?" he
asked.

"Nope," Sereeta replied. "I was hoping
some handsome dude would come along

and ask me out." She giggled. Jaris loved to hear her giggle. For a very long time, when her mom had been struggling with alcohol, Sereeta had felt unloved and abandoned. She'd rarely smile, much less giggle. At one particularly bad time, she even cut herself to ease her mental pain.

"Well," Jaris responded, "I don't think that handsome dude is gonna show up. Maybe you'll settle for going to a nice little club with me? A little band is playing, friends of Oliver's. They play loud rocking music, just what you like, Sereeta. They were going nowhere for a while, but now they're getting a few club dates. There're two players. One's a white guy with red hair and a red beard. The other's a black guy with no hair and a nose ring and earrings."

"Sounds wonderful," Sereeta remarked. "What's the name of the band?"

"Life of Amphibians," Jaris said.

Sereeta laughed. "Perfect! You're on."

More customers started coming in then. Jaris and the rest of the workers at the

Chicken Shack got busy filling orders. Jaris managed to wave to Sereeta and her mother when they left.

By nine forty-five, things grew quiet. Neal grinned and commented, "Amberlynn, I think you're good for business. We got twice the business we usually get on Thursdays."

"Yeah," Jaris agreed. "It felt more like a Friday."

Jaris and Amberlynn began the end-of-day chores, wiping the tables clean and getting everything ready for the next day. All the people on the shift worked together smoothly, mostly in silence. Once in a while, Amberlynn asked Jaris a question. One was did he have any brothers or sisters?

"I got a little sister, a freshman at Tubman, Chelsea. I call her chili pepper 'cause she's a pistol," Jaris replied.

Amberlynn smiled. "She's lucky to have a big brother like you," she told him.

"I don't know about that," Jaris objected. "Sometimes I give her a hard time.

Our pop is real strict, and I kinda am too. I don't want some bad dudes messing with my little sister. Lot of them out there."

"Just the fact that you look after her like that says a lot about you," Amberlynn noted.

Jaris continued working. He was growing uncomfortable, and he wasn't sure why. Just then, Amberlynn turned to Jaris. He saw something in her eyes that made him even more nervous. Jaris knew that look. It was probably in his own eyes for years when he looked at Sereeta, loving her from afar. You couldn't mistake the look. Amberlynn liked him. He could tell, but he didn't want that. It was the last thing he wanted.

Jaris looked away, his mind spinning. He tried to tell himself it was nothing. Amberlynn just had a little crush on the guy who hired her. It was gratitude; that was all. He'd hired her. He'd driven her home. He'd been kind to her. It was only natural that she should feel something for him.

Jaris was tall and well built. He was building more muscle, jogging, and lifting weights. He wasn't a skinny little freshman or sophomore anymore. Jaris didn't think he was handsome, but he was. He had fine features and dark smoky eyes. He looked a lot like his father, who, going into middle age, was still handsome. Something about Jaris attracted girls. Alonee Lennox had loved him. So had others.

Yet Jaris used to be nervous and insecure. He'd thought he was a loser. His father had been the same way. It was hard for both of them to recognize their own good qualities.

Now Jaris was gaining confidence, and it showed. He was even more appealing when he took charge of serious situations and made things happen. Even last year he would never have been able to stop Mr. Myers on Highway 16. He could not have kept him from driving drunk onto the freeway. He probably would have been too frightened by the challenge. He would have ignored the dangerous situation and just hoped for the best. Now Jaris was stronger, more confident.

And now Amberlynn looked at him with a special look. Maybe it was just admiration; maybe it was more.

On Friday afternoon, the next day, Chelsea came home from school on her bike. Heston rode his bike alongside her. Chelsea burst into the house, screaming. "We're in! We're in! Me and Heston got the parts!"

Mom laughed when Chelsea flew into her arms, almost knocking her down. "Mom, I'm gonna play Harriet Tubman when she was a young girl like me," Chelsea bubbled. "The play is called *Courage* 'cause she was so brave. And Heston's gonna be the boy Harriet saved!"

Heston stood there smiling sheepishly. "It's gonna be fun," he added. "It's a big deal. That lady, Ms. Duvall, she wrote the play. She brought in people for costumes and music, and Mr. Wingate is all excited."

Pop was cooking spaghetti, but the rumpus in the living room drew him out. "Hey, little girl, you got it, huh. Good for you. You'll be a smash. C'mere." Pop crouched a little, arms open wide, and spaghetti sauce all over his apron.

Chelsea ran into her father's arms, oblivious to the sauce now on her pretty yellow top. Pop lifted Chelsea off her feet and hugged her. He swung her around and put her back down.

Then he turned to Heston. The boy had always been a little afraid of Mr. Spain. At the moment, the red spaghetti sauce on Pop's white apron looked a little like blood. Heston took a small step backward. Pop spoke to him. "And you got the part you wanted too. Huh, Heston? Where you get to go without your shirt on."

Heston became even more frightened than a moment ago. "*What*? Oh no, Mr. Spain," he gasped. "I always wear my shirt."

"That's good," Pop asserted. "See that you wear your shirt and everything else too. People look better in their clothes than without them. See, the reason animals look so nice without no clothes, they got this fur on their bodies. We ain't got no fur, hence we need to wear our clothes. Don't you agree, Heston?"

"Oh yes, sir," Heston agreed fervently.

Mom's pride and happiness at Chelsea's triumph started to give way to embarrassment. She turned to her husband and spoke in a low, tight voice. "Lorenzo, what on earth are you talking about?"

"Oh, babe," Pop explained, "the little girl was telling me the other day. See, this dude, Heston, he's—what did you call him, little girl? Yeah, a stud. Seems like in the play he's losing his shirt a lot, and our little girl is gettin' goose bumps. I don't know what's all goin' on with the shirt gettin' away from the boy. Maybe the slave chasers are grabbin' on to it. Maybe those mean dogs're pullin' off shirts or somethin'. But we gotta put a stop to that."

Mom looked horrified. At times like this, she believed she'd married a madman. Fortunately, such times were the exception rather than the rule, but she was still mortified when they happened. Mom looked at Chelsea and commented, "Your father is just joking, Chelsea. Heston, don't mind him. He has such a sense of humor."

Heston didn't believe for a moment that Mr. Spain was joking. He looked at Pop and spoke sincerely. "I have my shirt on all the time in the play, sir. It has some tears in it, but it's always on."

"Good for you, boy," Pop declared. "That's the way it oughta be. Want to stay for dinner, Heston? We're having spaghetti and meatballs. I mean the real stuff. We don't get our spaghetti and meatballs outta no jar. I make the pasta from scratch. I make the sauce. All my own ingredients. No stuffed shirt guy on a jar is gonna make my spaghetti."

Heston felt caught. He was genuinely fearful of this tall, strange man in the red stained apron and the puffy hat. On the other hand, the aroma coming from the kitchen was hard to resist—garlic, onions, herbs. Heston's growling stomach won over his trembling heart.

"Uh," he finally grunted, "I'll call home and see if I can stay." After a brief phone conversation with his mother, he smiled and said, "I can stay."

"All right," Pop ordered, "let's get ready to eat!" He led the way into the dining room like a strange, white-clad general. The red sauce on his tunic was perhaps from a recent battle. He was a tall, handsome, commanding figure.

That same night, Jaris picked up Sereeta at her grandmother's house, where she lived. Her grandmother had taken her in because Sereeta's mother had been having problems with drinking.

Jaris and Sereeta drove to the little club where Life of Amphibians was playing.

On the way, Jaris asked Serecta about her mother. "Your mom seemed really good when you guys came in the Chicken Shack. It looks like that rehab really worked for her."

"Yeah," Sereeta agreed. "Mom is so much better. She still has her insecurities and stuff, but she's handling them much better. Like when she's stressed, she'll drink some hot herbal tea and meditate. In fact, she's meditating now." Sereeta shook her head and went on. "Seeing that beautiful girl, that Amberlynn, kinda shook Mom up. All the way home, she kept saying how old she felt when she saw girls like that. And I'm telling her she's not old at all 'cause she isn't. But Mom wants to be seventeen again."

Sereeta paused and then spoke. "Amberlynn is really gorgeous. Trevor told me at school today that he's gonna try to make a date with her. Poor Trevor is so lonely since he broke up with Vanessa. You think he's got a chance with Amberlynn?"

Jaris shrugged. "Who knows?" he replied. "Probably not. Trevor's a great guy,
but he's a little out of his league with her.
She probably dates star football players
over at Lincoln."

"Jaris, just in the short time I was there
I noticed something." Sereeta was speaking
in her I-have-to-say-this tone. "Amberlynn
has her eye on you."

Jaris hated to hear Sereeta say that
because he had noticed the same thing.
Hearing Sereeta say it just confirmed his
suspicions.

"I guess she's grateful that I hired and
trained her," Jaris suggested lamely. "And
then one time I took her home because she
was gonna wait at the dark bus stop. I think
she's just, you know, grateful."

"No, it's more, Jaris," Sereeta insisted.
"You're a great-looking guy. But there's
more to it than that, and Amberlynn sees
it. She's a bright girl, and she sees a good-
looking guy who is incredibly special. That
appeals to her."

"I'm just an ordinary guy," Jaris objected quickly. "Believe me, I'm in no way special." Jaris felt as though he had to explain himself.

"You know," he went on, "my pop has always said life has dealt him some bad blows. He got cheated out of college and then stuck in a dead-end job. Pop's better now that he has his own garage, but he still sometimes sees the dark side and feels insecure. I'm the same way. It's so easy for me to feel like a loser. All the time I wanted to be with you, I thought it never would happen. I thought, 'How could a nobody like me get a girl so fantastic?' You seemed so out of reach, Sereeta."

He glanced over at his girlfriend. Her brow was creased, and her lips were pursed. The expression said, "So?"

"Well," Jaris continued, "even now, sometimes in the middle of the night, all the old darkness comes down on me. I start thinking I'll flunk AP American History, and I won't graduate with a good enough grade. Then I won't get to be a teacher, and maybe you won't like me anymore, and then I'll be lost."

"Jaris," Sereeta protested, "I hear what you're saying. But Amberlynn doesn't see any of that. I can't put my finger on what makes you so amazing. Maybe it's just knowing that, whatever happens, you'll do the right thing. You're just a very good person, Jaris, and that is so endearing. Sure, I love that you're so cute and sweet and have a good personality. And, of course, like Chelsea says about Heston, you're *ripped*, babe."

She reached over and gently squeezed Jaris's arm.

"But it's so much more," Sereeta continued. "I love you most of all because you're so incredibly *decent*. You're a lot like your father. He rants and raves, but he has such integrity. Like when Jasmine Benson was gonna run away with Zendon. You went over there without a moment's hesitation to stop her. To save her. You fought to save

Jasmine when you don't even *like* her. You were also helping Marko rescue his old girl-friend, and you almost *hate* Marco. No one knew it then, but Zendon was a murderer. If he'd gotten Jasmine to go with him, she might have lost her life. You were there for them, babe. You did the right thing."

"You were too," Jaris said softly.

"I was following your lead, Jaris," Sereeta objected. "I'm just saying that what appeals to Amberlynn is not just your good looks. There just aren't that many really special guys out there, and she's smart enough to recognize one when she sees him."

"Well," Jaris sighed, "she's a nice kid and a very good employee. I hope what you saw was just plain old-fashioned grat-itude. But if it's more and she tries to get involved with me, I'll just level with her. I don't want to hurt her, but I'll tell her. I'm hopelessly, permanently in love with the most beautiful girl in the world. Sorry, I'm not available."

Sereeta laughed. "Yeah, right, I'm the most beautiful girl in the world. Except for the couple hundred thousand who're a lot better looking than me."

Jaris pulled into the club parking lot and turned off the engine. "C'mere," he ordered. Sereeta giggled. Jaris took her in his arms, kissing her gently on her soft, full lips. "Every time I do that," Jaris said, "I think I've died and gone to heaven."

Guitar riffs and drum music floated from the club into the parking lot. "I guess we have to go inside," Jaris whispered, "but I'd rather stay here a while."

"We promised Oliver we'd see his friends and tell them how great they are," Sereeta reminded him.

"Just two more minutes," Jaris pleaded. He held his girl in his arms and kissed her creamy smooth, golden brown cheek.

CHAPTER SIX

Trevor Jenkins lived with his single mom, hard-nosed Mickey Jenkins. His older brother Tommy, who was attending community college, lived with them too. His two oldest brothers were in the United States Army.

Trevor always thought his brothers went into the army early partly to escape Ma's strict rules. Mickey Jenkins wasn't afraid to knot a wet towel and use it to beat any of her sons for their misdeeds. Lately, she had eased up on Trevor. But during the years when his mother disapproved of his having a girlfriend, Trevor was deeply lonely. Now that Ma thought he was old enough for a girlfriend, he couldn't get one. Vanessa, his first real love, turned out to be an addict and a criminal. Now he was hanging with Shay, but that wasn't working out either. Trevor and Shay just didn't click.

Trevor really liked Amberlynn Parson, and he was determined to try to be closer to her, maybe even become her boyfriend. She didn't talk about having a steady guy, so just maybe she was available.

Monday morning, Trevor and his brother were getting ready for school, and Trevor decided to ask for advice.

"Tommy," Trevor said, "Jaris hired this really hot chick at the Chicken Shack. She's a junior over at Lincoln. Man, she's so hot I'd be afraid to touch her. I wanna be her boyfriend, man. You got plenty of chicks, Tommy. How do you do it?"

Tommy laughed. "I'm better looking than you, dude," he replied. It wasn't true. They were both good-looking young men, athletic, and friendly. In fact, Trevor was the better-looking of the pair. Tommy was outgoing, sure of himself. Trevor tended to be shy. He feared he just wasn't cool, and girls caught on to that.

"Trev," Tommy answered seriously, "just hang in there. Chicks aren't like fruit. They don't just drop from the trees when they're ripe and ready for pickin', man. If you like this chick, keep after her. Look at Jaris. He's a hot sucka, and he had to work hard to get Sereeta. She couldn't see the guy for sour apples for a long time. But he kept going after her. Persistence. That's the deal."

"Amberlynn's her name," Trevor remarked, smiling a little. "Man, she's so hot. I already told her I'm on the track team and we got a meet on Wednesday. When Carissa Polson saw Kevin Walker running in the meets, she fell for him. I'm hoping Amberlynn comes and watches me run. But she didn't seem too interested. Tonight I'll be working the same shift as she is. I thought you'd have some tips for me, bro. I want this chick so bad."

"Here," Tommy suggested, "you can use my aftershave lotion. My girlfriend likes it."

"I'll try anything," Trevor said.

"Just be nice to her, Trev," Tommy urged. "Laugh a lot. Girls like happy guys. Make her laugh, dude." He threw an arm around his younger brother's shoulders. "You'll score eventually, man. Maybe not with this chick, but somewhere out there there's a babe for you. When you hook up with the right one, you'll know why it took so long 'cause you'll be walkin' on air."

Trevor felt better after talking to Tommy. His brother had reminded him of how it was when Jaris and Trevor were juniors. Jaris was eating his heart out over Sereeta. She didn't seem interested in him at all. Trevor remembered that Jaris had bought Sereeta golden earrings for her birthday. Trevor had tried to discourage him; he thought the gift was over-the-top. Why should a guy spend a lot of money on golden earrings for a chick who isn't interested in him? And, like

Amberlynn, Sereeta was and is a beauty. Trevor remembered thinking she was way out of Jaris's league.

But, as Tommy said, Jaris didn't give up. He kept on trying to win Sereeta, and they ended up falling in love. Now no couple on Tubman's campus were closer than Sereeta and Jaris. Trevor's hopes rose. Things could be like that with him and Amberlynn. If he was just patient and persistent he could maybe win her over.

Later that same morning, Chelsea and her friend Inessa Weaver were walking onto the Tubman campus. They stopped at the statue of Harriet Tubman. Chelsea had often glanced at the statue of the plain woman in her simple homespun clothes. Chelsea knew she was a selfless, brave woman who had led many slaves to freedom. She had risked her life for others. But Chelsea had never looked at the statue as intently as she did this morning. Now she had been chosen to play Harriet in *Courage*.

"Look, Inessa," Chelsea whispered in a suddenly awed voice. "There she is. Oh, I'm so honored to be playing her. Y'know what I'm saying? Last night, Athena let me use her cool new phone, and I tweeted everybody with the good news. I texted kids too."

"Isn't Athena mad that she didn't get the role?" Inessa asked.

"Oh, she's gonna be in the play too," Chelsea explained. "But she really didn't want to be Harriet 'cause it's a lot of work portraying the lead. Athena said she's got more fun things to do than that."

Just then, Kanika Brewster came along. She had tried out for the Harriet Tubman role too, but she badly flubbed her lines.

"What're you doing standing there gawking at the statue of Harriet Tubman for, Spain?" Kanika remarked bitterly. "Ain't you ever seen that statue before? *I* deserved to play her, you know. Only reason you got the part was that you cheated like you always do."

"I cheated?" Chelsea asked in astonishment. "What are you talking about? We all had our chance to read for the part. Mr. Wingate and Ms. Duvall picked me 'cause I was the best."

"Don't play Miss Innocent with me, Spain," Kanika snarled. "All your creepy little friends were sitting there in the auditorium during the tryouts. When it was my turn to read and I slipped on one little word, they were all making faces and laughing. That made me nervous, so I made some more mistakes. You planned it all. You did it on purpose. I got your number, girl. You were part of it too, Inessa. Keisha and Falisha too. I hate you all."

"Kanika Brewster," Inessa protested in a shrill voice, "Mr. Wingate said that anyone who made *any* noise during the tryouts would be in big trouble. I was sitting with Keisha and Athena and Falisha when you were reading. We didn't even whisper."

"Yeah, but you made faces!" Kanika insisted.

"*We did not!*" Inessa hissed. "You're just a sore loser, that's all. You lost fair and square, and Chelsea won!"

"I'm telling everybody what you did to me, Spain, you and your dirty friends," Kanika threatened. "When I get done, you won't have a friend left at Tubman. I'll fix you. Hana Ray saw the whole thing. She said you were all making faces and that threw me off, and I lost 'cause of that."

Chelsea chimed in. "You were prancing around on the stage with your hands on your hips when you tried out for Harriet Tubman. That's why you lost. You made her out to be some little twit from dancing school instead of a poor slave girl. You were tossing your head and smiling like you were at a beauty pageant or something. Nobody laughed and nobody made faces, but everybody thought you were awful!"

When Kanika walked away, Inessa shook her head. "What a little creep she is," she remarked. "She was the worst one who read for the part. Nobody likes her anyway. She's so stuck-up, and she's always talking trash about somebody."

Later, in Ms. Colbert's class, Chelsea and the other students were looking through microscopes at slides. Two students at each microscope took turns looking at the slide and making notes. Chelsea was working with a girl named Cee-Ann. Cee-Ann wasn't a friend of Chelsea's, but they'd talked a few times during lunch and breaks. Cee-Ann always seemed pretty nice.

"Look, Cee-Ann," Chelsea noted, "all the bubbles … "

Cee-Ann raised her hand. "Ms. Colbert, could I have a different partner, please? Chelsea is talking all the time and disturbing me."

Ms. Colbert looked surprised. She knew Chelsea to be a good student. But she replied, "Chelsea, change places with Maurice. Maurice, you can be Cee-Ann's partner. And, everybody, no unnecessary talking."

Chelsea was shocked at what Cee-Ann had done. Then she remembered what Kanika had threatened to do. Chelsea could hardly wait until the class ended. Outside, she caught up to Cee-Ann. "Cee-Ann, why did you do that?" Chelsea demanded. "I wasn't talking, and you made me look bad in front of Ms. Colbert."

Cee-Ann gave Chelsea a dirty look and walked away. The same thing happened to Chelsea a few more times during the day. Kids she normally said "Hi" to snubbed her.

Chelsea knew what was happening. Kanika was trying to make Chelsea's life so miserable that she'd be sorry she won the part of Harriet Tubman. Kanika wanted to freeze Chelsea out completely. The plan might have worked when freshman class was first underway and few friendships were formed. But now it was too late. Chelsea already had too many friends, and Kanika didn't have that many. She just didn't have that much influence.

At lunchtime, Athena, Falisha Colbert, Inessa, and Keisha Knight joined Chelsea, as usual, under the pepper trees. Chelsea told them what had happened.

"Just ignore it, girl," Athena urged with a shrug. "Only kids being mean to you are friends with Kanika. If they're Kanika's friends, who needs 'em? She's nasty, and all her friends are nasty."

Maurice and Heston came to join the girls. Maurice grinned at Chelsea and told her, "Hey, Chelsea, I been told not to talk to you today. Some ugly chick told me that, and I blew her off."

"Kanika Brewster," Chelsea replied. "She's telling everybody me and my friends spoiled her audition for *Courage*. So I got the part of Harriet instead of her."

"I was there the whole time," Heston commented. "Kanika was really bad in the tryouts. She was like trying out for a musical revue or something. Nobody made faces and laughed when Kanika was up there trying out, but we sure felt like it."

"Yeah," Keisha added, "can you imagine if Kanika Brewster was picked to play Harriet Tubman? I think old Harriet woulda jumped off her pedestal and chased Kanika with a broom. That selfish girl got no right to play a beautiful lady like Harriet."

Everyone chuckled at that image and then fell silent. After a short while, Heston spoke up.

"You know, Chelsea? That was the best spaghetti I ever had in my whole life, at your house, you know."

Chelsea smiled. "Pop's a good cook. Mom hardly cooks at all 'cause she's busy with her classes and checking homework. She used to buy these frozen dinners in the cardboard boxes. We'd pop them in the oven, and it all tasted the same. The chicken nuggets tasted just like the fish stuff. We had to look at the box to see what we were eating. Was it chicken, beef, mystery meat?"

Chelsea noticed that Heston was smiling at her a lot. All the time she was eating her sandwich, he was just looking at her.

Chelsea had been afraid that all Pop's ranting about the torn shirt would scare Heston off. But it didn't seem to have bothered him.

"I love to watch you eat, Chelsea," he commented. "It's so cute how you lick off all the mustard."

After lunch, Chelsea and Heston walked across the campus together to their next class.

"You're nice, Chel," Heston told her. "It's gonna be so fun working on the play with you, all those practices—"

"You're nice too, Heston," Chelsea responded, turning and looking at him. Then Chelsea burst into giggles.

"*What*?" Heston asked.

"Did you wonder why Pop was going on so about your shirt, Heston?" Chelsea asked.

"Yeah, I kinda wondered about that, but I didn't dare ask," Heston admitted.

"It was *my* fault, Heston," Chelsea explained. "I was telling Pop about your good strong voice and how you'd be great in the play. Then I told him I saw you in that old torn shirt. I sort of said I got goose bumps when I saw how good your muscles and your shoulders looked. I told him how cut you are."

Heston stared at Chelsea, a smile dancing on his lips. "You think?" he asked.

"What?" Chelsea said.

"That I look good?" he replied. "I mean, I've been pumping iron and stuff. You think it's working?"

"It's working for me," Chelsea giggled.

Heston was silent for a moment and then said, "Wow!"

"Huh?" Chelsea said.

"Oh man!" Heston sighed, grinning. He had more spring in his step as they walked on. They were going to be late for math. Heston grabbed Chelsea's hand, and they ran to the classroom. Chelsea got all goose bumpy again.

All that same day, Trevor spent very little time thinking about math or English or history. His thoughts were about going to work tonight at the Chicken Shack and asking Amberlynn for a date. Tommy had loaned Trevor his Cavalier, and after school, Trevor got it washed. He thought it would be super cool to pull up in his own car. He didn't plan to say it belonged to his brother. Not yet anyway.

Trevor was going to ask Jenny to bow out of her offer to drive Amberlynn home tonight. Then Trevor could offer to do it. Driving Amberlynn home in the Cavalier would be the perfect time for asking the big question.

Before he left for the Chicken Shack, Trevor showered with a body wash that was supposed to have an irresistible masculine aroma. He used Tommy's aftershave lotion too. He was pulling out all the stops.

Trevor checked his closet and found a nice white T-shirt he'd never worn before. When he took off his yellow and white Chicken Shack shirt for the drive to Amberlynn's house, he wanted to look sharp. The T-shirt fit him just right, showing off his muscular upper body. He thought Amberlynn might notice that. Girls liked guys who were built.

Jaris was already there when Trevor arrived. Now that he was assistant manager, Jaris had to get there early to make sure the shifts were all filled. "Hey, Trevor," he greeted.

"Hey. Amberlynn here?" he looked around. He didn't see her.

"She's on the four thirty–nine thirty shift. She should be here any minute," Jaris answered.

"I really like that girl, Jaris," Trevor confided.

"She's a nice kid and pretty too," Jaris agreed. He hoped Amberlynn and Trevor got to be friends. That would be a relief to Jaris. He wouldn't have to worry about her trying to cozy up to him.

"Doesn't she sorta get to you too, Jaris?" Trevor asked. "I mean, I know you love Sereeta. But just between you and me, how can any guy ignore a chick like Amberlynn?"

120

"I'm not dead yet, Trevor," Jaris admitted. "Yeah, I noticed, but she doesn't appeal to me."

Trevor changed into his yellow and white Chicken Shack shirt. "I'm hoping to get somewhere with her, Jaris," he declared. "I bet you think I'm outta my mind."

"Go for it, man," Jaris encouraged him. "But just don't harass her on the job. We don't want somebody sayin' we harass chicks around here."

Trevor laughed. "Got it."

Amberlynn came in wearing skinny jeans and a bright red halter top. "Hi, Jaris, Neal," she nodded. Then she paused, "And Trevor, right?"

"Yeah," Trevor said, smiling broadly at her. She looked even more beautiful than the last time he saw her.

The customers started coming in, including many from Tubman High. Marko Lane came in alone, without Jasmine. The last time he was in, Jasmine had dragged him off quickly before he got a good look at Amberlynn.

Marko climbed onto a stool and remarked, "Hey, babe, you are eye candy."

Trevor felt like punching Marko in the face. He had no business coming on to Amberlynn like that. He was such a jerk. He was a twenty-four-seven jerk. He never quit.

"What would you like?" Amberlynn asked.

"I want some of that iced coffee, babe," Marko ordered. "But I like it sweet, so would you stick your little finger in it to make it extra sweet?"

"It comes already sweetened," Amberlynn responded coolly. She acted as if Marko was a civilized customer instead of an idiot. "What size coffee?"

"Supersized like that bod of yours, babe," Marko quipped.

Jaris walked over to Marko and gave him a hard look. "Dude, knock it off. We don't allow customers to harass our people."

"Harass?" Marko gasped. "I'm giving the chick compliments."

Jaris turned to Amberlynn, "Go help those two girls who just came in," he told her. "I'll bring this moron his iced coffee."

"It's all right, Jaris," Amberlynn objected. "I'm fine."

"I know," Jaris said but got the coffee anyway.

Jaris brought the iced coffee to Marko. "What's the matter, sucka," Jaris asked through gritted teeth. "Jasmine on vacation or something?"

"I get around on my own sometimes," Marko answered. "She ain't got me on no leash, if y'know what I'm sayin'."

"Jasmine said something about her mother making her go visit her grandmother in the nursing home," Jaris commented. "That's where she is, right?" He'd heard Jasmine bitterly complaining at school. She had to visit her grandmother who didn't even know who she was anymore. So what was the sense of visiting her, she wanted to know.

Marko shrugged. "So the cat's away. So what?"

Amberlynn looked at Jaris. She was impressed. He had quickly come to her rescue when that boy was making unwelcome comments. Amberlynn wondered whether that meant anything. Did Jaris like her, or was he just being a good manager? Amberlynn hoped it meant he was getting to like her.

Trevor got Jenny to switch with him in taking Amberlynn home. As quitting time neared, Trevor's heart began to race with hope and dread.

"Hey, Amberlynn," Trevor said with a friendly smile. "Jenny asked me if I could take you home tonight. I guess she has to go somewhere else. Is that okay?"

"Oh," Amberlynn responded. "You sure I won't be putting you out, Trevor? I can always take the bus."

"No, no!" Trevor insisted. "I'd like to drive you."

Jaris watched the exchange. He knew Trevor had connived with Jenny to get this chance. He just hoped it would be a success. Trevor was a good guy, and he was very lonely. He deserved a nice girlfriend. And if Amberlynn got to like Trevor, she would stop giving Jaris those strange looks that made him so nervous.

CHAPTER SEVEN

As Amberlynn walked out of the Chicken Shack with Trevor, she spotted the Cavalier right away. "Oh, do you drive that Cavalier, Trevor?" she asked.

"Yeah, I love it," Trevor answered.

"It's a cool car," Amberlynn commented. Trevor knew it wasn't cool. She was just being kind. He held the passenger-side door open for Amberlynn as she got in. He closed it when she was in. Ma taught him good manners. You open doors for girls, and when you pick them up, you knock on their doors. You didn't sit out front and honk your horn, as some dudes did.

"You a senior at Tubman too, like Jaris?" Amberlynn asked.

"Yep," Trevor nodded. "I been looking forward to being a senior for a long time. I guess we all do that. It seemed like junior year lasted forever."

"That's what I'm going through now," Amberlynn said. "I'm a junior at Lincoln. I'm going for my driver's license, but there's no money for getting me a car. My parents were going to loan me money for a cheap car, but then my dad got laid off. He's in construction, and you know what happened there. One day they were putting up houses all over the place, and the next day the market busted."

"Yeah," Trevor agreed, "that's tough."

"What does your father do, Trevor?" she asked.

Trevor froze. His father had abandoned the family when Trevor was a baby. His mother had struggled to raise her four boys alone on a nurse's aide salary. Trevor's father, Harry Jenkins, stumbled around the streets asking for change for a cup of coffee. He slept behind thrift stores and fished through dumpsters for empty cans and bottles to redeem. Trevor was deeply ashamed of his father, but he didn't want to lie to this girl. If he got lucky and they became close friends, she would need the truth. It would be painful to admit he had lied in the very beginning.

"My parents haven't been together for a long time," Trevor confessed. "Ma raised me and my three brothers all by herself. She works at a nursing home, and she sometimes puts in three shifts to keep it going. I'm really proud of her for raising us like she has. I got two brothers in the U.S. Army and one going to community college. I'm going to college too when I graduate Tubman. Ma is awesome."

"You bet she is," Amberlynn agreed. "What a brave and wonderful lady."

"Ma's real proud of us," Trevor continued. "She's got pictures of my brothers in their army uniforms on the wall. She's got pictures of Tommy, my brother in college, when he graduated high school. She's got a space saved for me in my Tubman graduation gown." Trevor was pleased that the girl seemed impressed.

Then Amberlynn asked, "Are you and Jaris close friends?"

"Yeah, we've known each other since we were little kids," Trevor told her. "We used to skateboard together and play ball, hang out." He wondered why Amberlynn brought up Jaris. Did she like him? Was that it? Was she fishing for information on him because she thought he was hot? Trevor's heart began to sink. Given the choice, most chicks would prefer Jaris over Trevor. Trevor knew that.

"Jaris is really nice," Amberlynn noted. "When he trained me, he was so patient."

"He's a great guy, yeah," Trevor agreed carefully. "He's my best friend. We'd do anything for each other. Me and him belong to this little group of seniors at Tubman. We call it 'Alonee's posse' 'cause a girl name Alonee Lennox sorta brought us together. We always eat lunch together, and we got each other's backs. Y'know what I'm sayin'?"

"Yeah, that's very nice," Amberlynn replied. "Is Alonee Jaris's girlfriend?"

She was fishing all right, Trevor realized. She wanted to know whether he was available. She wondered if the coast was clear to go after him.

"No," Trevor answered, "Alonee's just a friend. But Jaris does have a girlfriend. Her name's Sereeta. Jaris is crazy about her. He said he fell for her when he was just a kid in middle school. But they didn't start going together till they were juniors."

Trevor carefully watched the dark, narrow road ahead of them. But he snatched a quick look at Amberlynn's face to check her reaction to what he'd just told her. She didn't show any strong reaction. The pleasant smile remained on her face. Trevor wondered what that meant. Did she perhaps not really care for Jaris? Or did she not believe what Trevor just told her?

"I bet you got a boyfriend at Lincoln too, huh, Amberlynn?" Trevor probed. "Pretty girl like you?"

"Thanks, Trevor, but I don't," Amber-lynn answered. "I go out a lot, but with different guys. I just go out to have fun, nothing serious. Mom says that's good. She says that at my age I shouldn't get serious about any one guy."

Then she pointed forward. "Oh," she nodded, "the mobile home where I live is just ahead, after the gas station. We have a mobile home on Woodland Lane."

They were almost there. Trevor's opportunity to ask her out was rapidly slipping away. He got nervous. He had planned to ask her out, and this was it. They didn't know each other well at all, but still he planned to ask her out. If he was going to do it, he had to do it quickly.

"You like movies, Amberlynn?" Trevor asked.

"Yeah, I love sci-fi, lots of special effects," she replied.

"There's a new sci-fi movie at the mall. I was thinking of going to see it Saturday night," Trevor ventured. "It's supposed to have really awesome special effects. That sorta makes or breaks a movie like that, huh?"

Amberlynn was silent.

"Uh," Trevor asked, "would you like to come with me, Amberlynn?"

There, he had done it. His heart was pounding. His hands were clammy on the steering wheel. He was glad he put on heavy-duty deodorant because he was sweating all over.

"No thanks, Trevor," Amberlynn answered matter-of-factly. "I'm going to be busy Saturday night. Thanks for asking me, and thanks for the ride home too. I hope it wasn't too much trouble for you." She got out of the car, closed the door, smiled, and waved to him before she walked to her door. At the door, she turned again and called out, "Night, Trevor!" Then she went in.

Trevor sat there at the wheel of the car, his mouth dry. He felt let down. He felt like an idiot. He had asked her too soon. He should have waited until they knew each other better. He berated himself for asking her out when they were still strangers. She must have thought he was crazy. Why did he make a fool of himself like that? Trevor pressed his forehead on the steering wheel and told himself, over and over, that he was stupid. Then he backed out of the driveway and drove off into the night, heading home.

Amberlynn rushed into the mobile home. Mom was still up. "Dad went to bed," Mom explained. "He got some work today, and he's completely worn out. They're putting a new roof on a house, and he was up and down those ladders all day. In this heat. I'm really worried about him. How was your day, honey?"

"Good, Mom," the girl replied. "Some creepy guy came in the Chicken Shack and really came on to me. You shoulda seen Jaris take him on. Jaris put that dude in his place fast." Amberlynn had a dreamy look on her face.

"That wasn't Jaris who just brought you home, was it, Amberlynn?" Mom asked.

"I didn't recognize the car. Doesn't Jaris have a Honda?"

"Yeah, you're right, Mom," Amberlynn answered. "Another guy who works at the Chicken Shack brought me home. Trevor. He's sweet. He's a nice, dorky guy. I felt kinda bad. He asked me out, and I told him I was busy Saturday night. He's not my type at all, but I could tell he really likes me. It was awkward."

She disappeared for a moment into the kitchen. She put a bag of leftover fried chicken pieces into the fridge.

"I'm pretty sure Jaris likes me too," she continued as she came back to the living room. "The way he rushed to put that creep in his place tonight. Jaris is looking out for me. Trevor told me Jaris is real tight with a girlfriend, but I don't believe it. I think Trevor was trying to get my mind off Jaris so I'd be interested in him. Poor Trevor, he's kinda dumb. I could tell he was thinking real fast. He was just trying to convince me that Jaris is really into this other girl. But I can tell Jaris likes me a lot."

Mom smiled. "Well, honey, don't get your hopes up too high. You've only known this Jaris for a few days, and you really don't know what he's like."

"I feel like I've known him for a lot longer, Mom," Amberlynn objected. "I even had a dream about him last night. I dreamed we were dancing! He was such a good dancer. It was the most exciting dream." Amberlynn spun around the room in a happy twirling motion. Then she sank into the couch beside her mother. "I never met a guy I felt like this about, Mom. Never."

Trevor parked his brother's car and went inside the house. He felt as though he'd just been run over by a truck. Tommy heard him and called through the partition that divided a small bedroom into two even smaller rooms. "How'd it go, dude?"

"It was a car crash, man," Trevor replied. "She just can't see me." He sat down on his lumpy bed and put his face in his hands.

Tommy peered around the corner. "Man, don't freak. Be patient," the brother advised. "The chick hardly knows you. Just keep on trying. She might come around."

"Nope," Trevor insisted. "Chicks don't like me. Vanessa didn't even like me. She just went out with me 'cause she wanted to use me, man. She wanted some dope to help her and her crooked friends pull off jobs. That's the only reason Vanessa Allen hung with me. She thought, 'Here's some-body who looks pretty stupid. We could get him to drive a getaway car or do just about anything else we tell him to do.'"

"Trev, you're feeling low right now, but it can all change," Tommy asserted. "If it doesn't work out with this chick, there'll be another one along in a minute. And she'll be just right for you. Trust me. Somewhere out there, there's one for you."

"Thanks for trying to cheer me up, Tommy," Trevor grumbled. "But I'll never get a girlfriend. I'm gonna try to get some sleep now."

Trevor thought of his mother, his poor, worn-out mother. She had once confessed that was never a pretty woman and that boys didn't like her. They liked the pretty chicks. So Ma settled for Harry Jenkins even though she knew he was no good.

Trevor felt like kicking himself from one end of the room to the other. How could a jerk like him have thought that somebody as hot as Amberlynn would go for him? Now he was even embarrassed to show up for work when he and Amberlynn had the same shifts. Every time she looked at him, she'd be thinking, "Oh, there's that poor fool who asked me to go to the movies with him. Like I'd go anywhere with some- body like that. Please don't let him ask me again."

Trevor flopped back on his bed and tried to sleep.

CHAPTER EIGHT

Usually, Chelsea and Inessa walked home from school together. But today, Chelsea and Heston had stayed late for rehearsal, and they walked home together. It was a cool, sunny day, and they walked slowly. They talked about the play, about classes they shared, and finally about the strange site on Iroquois Street. "Did you ever see the burned-out house on Iroquois Street, Heston?" Chelsea asked.

"No," Heston replied.

"Come on," Chelsea suggested. "Let's walk by there. It's not gonna be dark for a while. We'll get home in plenty of time."

About halfway to Iroquois Street, Heston reached out and took Chelsea's hand. Chelsea thought his hand was big and strong, and she liked him holding her hand. She could walk just about anywhere and not be afraid as long as Heston was holding her hand.

"It's behind the old pizza place," Chelsea explained. "Look, there's pepper trees there and the foundation stones of a house that burned down years ago. Everybody died in the fire."

"That's sad," Heston remarked as they drew closer.

"My brother's girlfriend, Sereeta," Chelsea said, "she said it's peaceful there. She said you could feel the spirits of the people who died in the fire. They were very sad before they died, but then they were peaceful. She said they're happy now."

As they drew closer, Heston tightened his grip on Chelsea's hand, and he stiffened. "Somebody over there sitting on the foundation stones. See?"

"Yeah, I see," Chelsea replied.

"I think it's a guy," Heston noted. "His head is down. He's bent over, and he's resting his head in his hands. I don't think we should get any closer, Chelsea. He looks like he feels really bad about something. I think he wants to be left alone."

Chelsea squinted her eyes for a better look. "I think I know him, Heston," she said. "That's my brother's friend, Trevor Jenkins."

"Yeah?" Heston nodded. "Yeah, I've seen him around school with the seniors. Is something wrong with his family or something?"

"I don't know," Chelsea responded. "Let's get out of here before he sees us. I don't want him to know that we saw him. He might feel bad. He's really nice, Heston. He's my brother's best friend."

They turned and walked down Iroquois Street toward where Chelsea lived. The street was quiet now, as dusk gathered around them. It was a peaceful time of day with few sounds. They heard only a few distant yelps from dogs, and some children playing on skateboards on the next street. The sounds were muted.

"Trevor seems kind of lonely sometimes," Chelsea commented.

"Yeah? Poor guy," Heston responded.

"All Jaris's guy friends have girlfriends, but he doesn't," Chelsea went on. "He had a girlfriend once, but she turned out to be a bad person. She's in jail now. Trevor was happy when they were going together, and what happened really took him down."

"Look," Heston nodded toward the setting sun. "The sky is turning all pink and blue. I guess it'll be dark pretty quick now."

"We better hurry," Chelsea urged.

Heston tightened his grip on Chelsea's hand. He touched her shoulder and turned her toward him. He bent down and kissed her real fast. It was quick, but tender. To Chelsea, the kiss felt as though a butterfly had landed on her lips, then flew away. Neither of them said a word, but their hands were still joined. They jogged toward Chelsea's house and got there well before dark, while swaths of pink and blue were still in the graying sky.

Chelsea smiled at Heston. She turned and ran up her walk. He jogged toward his own house a few blocks away. Chelsea stood at the door for a moment before going into the house. She reached up with her fingers and touched her lips. She felt unreasonably happy. She was feeling bombarded by many wild, conflicting, delightful, and scary emotions. She couldn't remember a moment in her life when she had felt like that.

When Chelsea went in the house, Jaris was working on the computer.

"Hi, Jare," Chelsea called out.

Jaris stopped working, turned, and smiled at his sister. "What happened?" he asked her.

"Huh? Nothing," Chelsea responded.

"You got stars in your eyes, chili pepper," Jaris commented.

"Me and Heston had a nice walk home," Chelsea explained "He's really, really nice."

"Uh-oh," Jaris sighed.

"What's that for?" Chelsea asked.

Jaris grinned. "Nothin', chili pepper. Heston *is* a good guy," he agreed.

"Jaris," Chelsea said, " 'member those foundation stones of the house that burned down a long time ago on Iroquois Street? Me and Heston saw Trevor sitting there. He looked so sad. He was holding his face in his hands. His elbows were resting on his knees. He looked like he was gonna cry or something. Heston and me got out of there. We didn't want him to see us looking at him."

"Oh brother, poor guy," Jaris groaned, getting up from the computer. Jaris knew Trevor had been angling for a date with Amberlynn. He apparently struck out.

Trevor had been going downhill ever since he had to walk away from Vanessa Allen. Under the eucalyptus trees at lunch-time with his friends, he'd be by himself. The other guys usually had their girls with them. Trevor was so painfully alone.

IF YOU WERE MINE

Jaris thought for a few minutes. Then he got on his cell phone. He remembered Kevin Walker saying he sometimes went to see professional fights on the weekends. His girlfriend, Carissa, hated boxing, so she didn't go with him. "Hey, Kevin, going to the boxing matches this weekend?" Jaris asked.

"Yeah," Kevin answered, "there's a real good Mexican welterweight on the card."

"Who's goin' with you, man?" Jaris asked.

"Far as I know, nobody," Kevin replied. "Boxing isn't as popular as it used to be. Just bloodthirsty dudes like me goin'. Why?"

"I'd like to go," Jaris told him.

"*You*, Jaris? Really?" Kevin gasped. Jaris could see Kevin laughing to himself. He had to be thinking Jaris had slipped a gear or something.

"Me and probably another guy, Kevin, okay?" Jaris confirmed. "I'll let you know. It'd be kinda fun for just us guys to take in a

144

fight. We could stop for some greasy burgers on the way home in some noisy dive."

"You make it sound like so much fun!" Kevin responded. "Lemme know."

Jaris then punched in the numbers of Trevor's cell phone. "Hey, man, what's hap'nin'?" Jaris asked.

"Nothin', dude. Same-old-same-old," Trevor answered in a dispirited voice.

"Me and Kevin gonna go to a boxing match on Saturday night," Jaris told him. "Then we're stopping for some greasy hamburgers in some dive on the boulevard. Remember when we were in middle school, and we'd do stupid guy stuff? That was before we met up with chicks who tamed us down. Man, they just take all the fun out of being rowdy. Wanna come, Trevor?"

There was a short pause. Then Trevor answered, "Well, it's the best offer I had this week. In fact, it's the *only* offer I had this week. So yeah."

"Okay, Trevor," Jaris told him. "I'll pick you up in my car around seven, and you and me and Kevin can have some fun. The last time I went to a fight was when I was ten. Pop took me, and Mom really freaked because I seemed to enjoy it too much. I think it appealed to my dark side."

Jaris called Kevin back. "Trevor Jenkins and I will be over a little after seven on Saturday. We'll ride down to the arena in my car. Okay, Kev?"

"Jaris," Kevin responded, "I can't tell you how glad I am that you've suddenly developed a taste for boxing. Why not, right? Seeing two guys bash each other to a bloody pulp in a smelly boxing ring. I mean, I'm a freak, so I like stuff like that, but *you*?"

Jaris knew Kevin was having fun with him.

"Uh-oh, hold on," Kevin went on. "Let me guess. Our friend Trevor is in a really bad place, right? He's goin' through a bad patch. Since that creep Vanessa went sour, he can't get a chick, and he's in the dumps.

So you want us to hang out with him to raise his spirits. How'm I doin' there, buddy?"

"Well, he's my friend, and I hate to see him so low. Do you think this is a stupid idea, Kevin?" Jaris asked.

"Dude, you are so goodhearted, you make me sick," Kevin told him. "But, lissen, knowin' somebody like you has our backs makes us all a lucky bunch of fools. I'll see you at seven. Nothin' like seeing another dude lying on the canvas bleeding to make a guy forget he has no chick on his arm." Kevin was laughing when he put down the phone.

On Saturday morning at breakfast, Jaris told everybody. "Me and Kevin and Trevor are going to a boxing match tonight at the arena."

"What?" Mom gasped. "Jaris, since when do you *like* that barbaric sport?"

"Well, I'm not crazy about it, Mom," Jaris admitted. "But Kevin likes it. And Trevor is so sad and lonely lately that we thought it would help to get his mind off things. Maybe an exciting boxing match'll give him a chance to let off some steam. Then we're going to some greasy spoon with dirty linoleum floors and eat super-sized burgers."

"Great idea," Pop exclaimed. "Good for you, boy, that you're looking out for your friends. Sometimes guys just have to get together and do guy stuff. And that's especially if their lives been messed up by some lousy chick, like what happened to Trevor."

"I think boxing is horrible," Mom declared. "It should be banned. Men pummeling each other, all bloody and bruised. I can't believe you're actually going to something like that, Jaris."

Pop laughed. "Hey, babe, I took the kid to a boxing match when he was ten or something. This one dude, he got punched so hard he come flying through the air. He almost landed in our laps. Remember that, Jaris?"

"Yeah, Pop," Jaris said. "His mouthpiece came flying through the ropes, and I got splashed with spittle!"

"Ohhh!" Mom groaned. "How gross!"

Pop had to go to his garage. He needed to take care of some Saturday customers who needed their cars for work on Monday. He put on his crisp green uniform with the red lettering on the pocket saying "Spain's Auto Care." Out he went, whistling.

As Pop drove his pickup down the street, he spotted Athena Edson and Chelsea riding their bikes. They were both in the middle of the street, weaving from side to side. Pop blasted the horn, and they scurried to the curb. He stopped alongside them and yelled out the window.

"Hey, hey, you're tryin' to ride bikes while you're texting or tweetin' or some other fool thing. You weavin' all over the road like drunks. If I'd been some jerk not watching out, I coulda run over you both."

Pop parked the pickup and got out. He looked at his daughter first. "Little girl," Pop growled, "you were ridin' that bike like an idiot. I thought maybe you got hold of some booze, and you were drunk or something. BUI. Bikin' under the influence."

Chelsea laughed and apologized. "I'm sorry, Pop, we were just callin' our friends and stuff. You know, telling them what we're up to."

"Stop laughin'," Pop commanded grimly. "It ain't no laughin' matter if a car hits a stupid kid on a bike who ain't payin' attention. And you, Athena, you're tweetin', right? Let's all tweet like the birdies tweet, right? Whole bunch of people out there can't wait till they hear every stupid thing you done today."

Pop was angry and on a roll. He stood with hands on hips and wagged his head as he spoke.

"Well, how's this for a tweet, airhead? 'I just got hit by a car, and I'm in the ICU. And they're trying to keep me alive, but

they ain't doin' so good.' That sound inter-
estin' enough for your airheaded friends?
You guys were swerving around like crazy.
I never seen such bad bike riding. You ain'
fit to ride trikes."

Both girls sobered quickly when they
saw Pop's rage.

"I'm sorry, Pop," Chelsea murmured.
"We just sorta forgot we were on the street,
I guess."

"Oh yeah, I understand that," Pop said,
pop-eyed with fury. "Was a kid about a
month ago on that hill on Pequot Street.
He forgot he was on the street too. He's
tellin' his friend about how good he done
in the soccer game. Oh, everybody cheerin'
and all that good stuff. Then he looks up,
and there's the grillwork of a Buick in his
face. He cusses, and that's it. That's the last
words he got out. They buried him three
days later." Pop took a step toward the two
girls. "Gimme those phones."

"But, Pop," Chelsea whined, "I need
my phone 'cause I gotta call the other cast

members in the play. You know, I have to touch base with them."

"Catch a pigeon and tie a note around its leg," Pop snapped. "Gimme the phone."

"Mr. Spain, you can't take my phone," Athena cried. "I need it desperately to—"

Lorenzo Spain grabbed Athena's phone. "I'll give it back to you maybe tomorrow, airhead," he said. "In the meantime, you get home, Chelsea. You put that bike in the garage, and you don't touch it again till I say so."

Pop got back in his truck with the phones and headed to his garage. "Stupid little idiots," Pop mumbled angrily to himself. Another car, perhaps a speeding car, could have come down that street instead of his truck. The thought turned him numb and sick. He was shaking. He was shaking with the realization of how quickly his child's life could have ended under a car. Just because of a text message she was busy sending or a car she missed seeing. It was an unforgiving world. A little mistake and a life could end in the blink of an eye.

Then Lorenzo Spain knew that his own life would be over as he knew it. If he lost any of them—Monica, Jaris, or Chelsea—he was not sure he could go on. The darkness would descend on him, and it might never lift again. He might keep going through the motions, but he wouldn't want to wake up in the morning anymore.

That night, Jaris picked up Kevin Walker and headed for Trevor's house. When he pulled in the driveway, he saw Trevor's mother pulling out in her old car. She was on her way to her job at the nursing home.

"Hey, boys!" she called out, a weary smile on her face. "I'm so glad you came. That boy has been so sorrowful. I'm so grateful you goin' someplace with m'boy. He missin' that bad girl, Vanessa, something awful. She no good for him, but now he got nothin'."

Deep lines appeared in Mickey Jenkins's brow, even though she wasn't that old. "Sometime I feel guilty, like I'm to blame," she went on. "I kept such a tight rein on that boy, he didn' have no chance to get his social life goin'. I didn' let him go out, you know, 'cause I thought he'd get in trouble. I was so afraid he'd get in trouble. But now it breaks my heart to see him so sad and lonely."

"He'll be okay, Mrs. Jenkins," Jaris assured her. "He's my best friend, and I know him. He'll be fine."

Mrs. Jenkins's smile deepened. "You're a finc boy, Jaris," she beamed. "I'm blessed that m'boy has you for a friend."

Trevor appeared then, coming out of the house. He had a faint smile on his face. "I ain't been to a boxing match in years," he admitted. "My uncle took me a long time ago, and it was exciting. Then I went with my brother Desmond one time, and I liked it."

"I went when I was ten with my pop," Jaris responded. "I thought it was great.

But this morning I told Mom that the guy's mouthpiece come flyin' out and I got spittle on me. She freaked. I thought Mom was gonna faint."

Trevor and Jaris laughed.

A few minutes later, they'd picked up Kevin.

"I love boxing," Kevin declared as he got into the car. "I've got so much anger in me. Seeing guys banging away on each other and getting away with it sorta releases all that." Kevin smiled and admitted, "I guess I'm my father's son."

"But he went too far," Jaris responded. "You won't. You got self-control."

Kevin's father had gotten into a fight with another man and killed him. He died in a prison riot while serving a long sentence. Kevin was just a toddler when it happened.

A lot of cars were arriving at the arena. Tacked all around the outside of the place were colorful posters of savage-looking fighters featured tonight. Little Juan Rodriguez was an up-and-coming welterweight. He hadn't lost a match yet. He was fighting Tiger Morales, who was a powerhouse in his own right. The bout promised to be a real brawl.

"I like welterweights the best," Kevin stated. "You get a lotta action. Sometimes the heavier guys are too cautious. They bob and weave through all the rounds, and it's a yawner."

The three boys went into the arena. The two preliminary bouts were not very exciting, but the boys were having fun hanging out together. Finally, the main-event fighters were standing in their respective corners. They were punching the air, practicing their footwork.

Jaris didn't know much about the boxing scene, so he asked, "Who do you like, Kevin?"

"Rodriguez," Kevin answered quickly. "It's his fight to lose. I don't know, though. Tiger's a scrappy guy."

"Tiger looks bigger than Rodriguez," Trevor said.

156

"Yeah, but Rodriguez is fast. I've seen him before. He has a smashing right," Kevin said.

When the bell rang for round one, the two men came out fighting. Clearly, Rodriguez was out for a quick knockout. He wanted to finish Morales off. He wasn't looking to win on points. He wanted Morales on the floor getting counted out.

Morales was a clever, courageous fighter. He dodged Rodriguez's blows, and by the fourth round it was pretty much an even fight. Rodriguez was slightly ahead on points, but the fight could go either way.

In the fifth round, Rodriguez went in for the kill. Kevin's face became animated as Jaris had rarely seen it. His eyes gleamed. He leaned over to Jaris, tapped him on the ribs, and predicted, "Here it comes, man."

With a series of battering rights, Rodriguez sent Morales sprawling into the canvas. Morales gamely tried to get up. He was on his knees. He looked dazed.

"The man has heart," Kevin remarked with obvious admiration.

Morales was counted out, and the fight was over. Jaris was relieved. He didn't need to see Morales pounded any more. Blood was running down his face. One eye was swelling shut. The referee raised Rodriguez's hand in victory, and Kevin was grinning happily. Even Trevor was excited and happy. The three boys cheered as Rodriguez marched around the ring, his gloved hands held aloft.

"Way to go, dude!" Kevin shouted as Rodriguez stepped from the ring. The boxer's cheeks were streaked with blood. Yet he smiled graciously and acknowledged the cheers of his fans, waving his hands in the air.

CHAPTER NINE

Now for the biggest, baddest burger in town, Kevin declared. He led the way from the arena into the darkness outside. "Onions, mayo, tomatoes, bacon, lettuce, cheese, salsa, olives maybe," he recited.

"The kitchen sink!" Trevor added, laughing. Jaris had not seen Trevor laugh in a while. Tonight was doing him some good, and Jaris was glad about that.

Jaris drove through the night in search of the best burger pit. They passed several possibilities, but Kevin just kept nodding no. He knew the perfect place.

"There it is," Kevin shouted. "George's Best Burgers. I've been there. I dislocated my shoulder lifting the burger."

The boys laughed as Jaris neared the burger joint. The parking lot was jammed with cars, and the restaurant was filled with customers, mostly guys. "They don't sell chick food," Kevin announced. "No dainty little salads with vinaigrette dressing. No healthy yogurt with cereal on the top. None o' them veggie burgers. Yech! This is red meat city. Double burgers, dressings oozing out the side. *Only man food sold here*."

The boys made "manly" grunting sounds as they emerged from the car.

Inside, the three giant hamburgers were finally delivered. The boys wolfed them down amid gulps from the giant soda cups.

"It's getting all over me," Jaris remarked.

"It's supposed to, dude," Kevin laughed.

"Man, this is good stuff," Trevor raved. "I didn't think stuff like this existed anymore. This is the best burger I ever had in my whole life."

"What did I say, man?" Kevin reminded him. "I wouldn't steer you wrong."

Jaris grinned as he chomped on his burger. He was happy the evening was a lift for Trevor. If Chelsea had not told Jaris about seeing Trevor so down, this night might never have happened. Jaris was so glad she told him. He knew Trevor was feeling low, but he didn't think it was so bad. Trevor needed this Saturday night. He needed it badly.

On Sunday, the phone rang at the Spain house at about eight thirty at night.

"Hey," Pop said, answering it.

"Mr. Spain, this is Trudy Edson, Athena's mother," an annoyed voice said.

"Yeah, I know who you are," Pop told the woman. "Wassup?"

"My daughter was biking with Chelsea earlier today," Mrs. Edson went on. "Somehow she left her expensive cell phone at your house and—"

"No, no, that's not what happened," Pop interrupted. "If your daughter told you that, Mrs. Edson, she's givin' you a fish story. Y'hear what I'm saying? What

161

happened is I confiscated her phone. The girls, your kid and mine, they were riding their bikes down the middle of the street. And they were weaving from side to side like drunks, busy on their cell phones textin' and tweetin'."

Pop was talking so rapid-fire that Mrs. Edson had no chance to say anything. "Little sports car fronta me hadda swerve to avoid 'em," Pop rattled on. "And I hadda swerve to keep from wipin' 'em out. I couldn't believe they'd do somethin' so dangerous. There they were, in the middle of traffic, not payin' any attention to anything but their stupid chitchat. So I took the phones away."

"Oh," Mrs. Edson said. She didn't sound surprised. Her daughter had probably told her the truth. She likely just wanted to avoid a confrontation with Mr. Spain by pretending that the phone was misplaced.

"Mr. Spain, Athena really needs her phone, so I thought perhaps I could come over—" Trudy Edson stammered.

Pop could hear Athena whining in the background. "Mommm, just get it!"

"I'll bring it over there on my way to work tomorrow," Pop declared. "In the meantime, you and your girl gotta have a talk about traffic safety. You don't want to be finding her under a truck 'cause she was tweetin' instead of lookin', Mrs. Edson. As for my kid, she ain't gettin' her phone back for a week and maybe not even then. See, Mrs. Edson, if that sports car didn't swerve, we might not be on the phone whining about missing cell phones. We might be planning a funeral for our little girls." Pop hung up.

"Who was that?" Mom asked.

"The airhead's idiot mother," Pop sneered. "Athena's whining about not havin' her cell phone 'cause I got it. I'm keeping it till tomorrow morning too. If the airhead wants to get in touch with her flaky friends, she can hire a carrier pigeon."

Mom stared at her husband. What Pop was doing embarrassed her. He had insulted Mrs. Edson, who was a high school teacher and Mom's fellow professional. They'd meet at various teachers' symposiums. Whenever the subject of Monica Spain's husband came up, Mrs. Edson got a funny look on her face. Still, Monica knew Lorenzo was right. The thought of Chelsea being hit on her bike sent chills through Monica's soul.

That same night, Trevor was working at the Chicken Shack, along with Jenny, Neal, and Amberlynn. Jaris didn't work. They would be together from late afternoon to the evening. Trevor still thought something good might happen between him and Amberlynn. She had turned him down for a date for Saturday night, but maybe she really did have other plans. The answer might not always be no.

Amberlynn smiled warmly at Trevor when they arrived at the Chicken Shack at about the same time. She had come on the bus.

"I coulda picked you up and brought you in," Trevor said.

"Oh, it's so easy to just get on the bus," Amberlynn replied.

"Yeah, but I'm taking you home tonight," Trevor told her. "Jenny's gettin' off early tonight. It's dangerous to wait at the bus stop in the dark. It's dangerous for any woman but especially for a pretty girl like you."

"Oh, thanks," Amberlynn said as she slipped on her yellow and white shirt.

Amberlynn looked around then and asked, "Jaris isn't working tonight, is he?"

"No," Trevor replied. "He doesn't work Sundays, but maybe he'll stop by. Sometimes he comes in with his girlfriend." Trevor wanted to make the point that Jaris had a girlfriend. He hoped that Jaris would come in with Sereeta. If Amberlynn had any ideas about Jaris, seeing those two together would wipe them out. She'd have no doubt how much they were into each other.

At nine fifteen, Jaris and Sereeta did come in. They ordered Chinese chicken salads and sat in a booth. Amberlynn took their orders and brought the salads. She smiled at Jaris and Sereeta. "Jaris did a really good job of training me here," Amberlynn told Sereeta.

"You were easy," Jaris said. "Real smart. Oh, Amberlynn, this is Sereeta Prince, my girlfriend. Sereeta, Amberlynn Parson is our new hire, and she's doing great."

"You guys both gonna graduate next June, huh?" Amberlynn asked. "I wish I was a senior too. I'm sick of high school. I suppose you'll be off to college then. You'll probably be going to different colleges?"

"No," Jaris answered. "We're both headed for the community college and then State. We don't have a lot of money, you know. We can get our units at community college at good prices. Then we'll get grants and head for State college." Jaris put his arm around Sereeta's shoulders. "No way I'd let this chick go to a different college. I gotta keep my eye on her."

Amberlynn's wide smile faded. She hurried off to take another order. Trevor was watching the whole thing, and he was overjoyed. Jaris left no doubt how he felt about Sereeta. Maybe, Trevor thought, later on might be a good time to ask Amberlynn out again. Surely she now realized that going for Jaris was futile.

Sereeta looked at Jaris and remarked, "You made her sad, Jaris."

Jaris shrugged. "I don't know if I did or not. But if she's got any wild ideas, now is the time to get rid of them."

"Jaris, I am so lucky," Sereeta told him. "I am so lucky to be with you. If I wasn't with you, I don't think I'd be with anybody. And to think, I didn't even like you that much at first. Now I can't imagine life without you."

"Babe," Jaris objected, "I'm the lucky one."

"No, really," Sereeta insisted. "Life is so weird. I've dated a lot of guys, and we've had fun, but nobody was ever like you. Without you, I'd be a jigsaw puzzle with one piece missing. There would always be a piece missing."

Amberlynn watched Jaris and Sereeta leave, holding hands as they went out the door. Jenny was standing nearby, watching Amberlynn watching the couple. Amberlynn had a wistful look on her face. Jenny came over and said, "You got the hots for him, huh?"

"Yeah," Amberlynn admitted. "But he's in love with that girl. And she's in love with him, right?"

"Yeah," Jenny affirmed. "I've been working here for two years. I knew Jaris before he and Sereeta got close. But he was in love with her even then. She was all he ever thought about. I never saw two like them once they got together. It's kind of a real love story, I guess."

Amberlynn nodded. "Just my luck," she mumbled.

"Hey, girl," Jenny advised, "I'll tell you somebody who'd like to take you out. Trevor Jenkins. He's a good friend of Jaris's, and he likes you a lot. He's a good kid. You wouldn't go wrong going out with him."

"He's not my type, Jenny," Amberlynn replied.

"Too bad," Jenny commented. She returned to making salads for the rush that often came just before closing on Sunday nights.

Trevor was plotting all during his shift what he might say to get Amberlynn's interest. She had said she liked sci-fi movies. Trevor knew a guy in town who collected *Star Wars* and *Star Trek* memorabilia. He was an eccentric, and he loved to show off his stuff. He went to all the Trekkie conventions and to Comic-Con.

When it was time for Trevor and Amberlynn to walk to Tommy's car after work, Trevor told her about his friend. "He's got posters and even life-sized characters. Maybe this weekend you'd like to see his stuff. Later on, we could get something to eat."

"I'm pretty busy with homework on the weekends," she answered.

"Everything okay, Amberlynn?" Trevor asked her as he started the car.

"Yeah," she said, staring out the window.

"You like old vintage cars?" Trevor asked.

"Sometimes," she murmured in a listless voice.

"Car club gets together on Wednesday night. They got these great muscle cars, and they got a rock band playing this Wednesday. Life of Amphibians. My friend Oliver Randall likes that band a lot. Maybe you'd like to go—"

"No, I've got some other stuff to do," Amberlynn interrupted.

Trevor gripped the wheel tighter in frustration. If Jaris didn't have a girlfriend, he could ask Amberlynn to look at interesting fence posts. She'd jump at the chance. She just didn't want to be with Trevor. No girl wanted to be with Trevor. The one girlfriend he had, Vanessa Allen, didn't even want him for himself. She was like all the other girls. She couldn't have cared less for Trevor, but he had been useful to her.

They were nearing Amberlynn's mobile home park. Trevor glanced over at her. "You seem really down. Anything I can do to help?" he asked her. "We could stop off and have a mocha at the Coffee Camp."

"No, that's okay. I'm fine," Amberlynn responded, gripping her purse. She couldn't wait to be out of the car and away from Trevor. The moment the car stopped, she jumped out.

"Thanks for the ride." She tossed the words over her shoulder as she ran toward her door.

Trevor could only imagine what she was saying to her parents right now. "Oh, what a night! That cute guy I really like—Jaris— turns out he's hooked up with another girl. Then this lame bozo, Trevor, was hinting about a date all the way home!"

Trevor headed home, feeling even bleaker than before.

On Monday morning, Pop waited until Chelsea had finished breakfast. Then he said, "Well, little girl, what's it gonna be, your bike or your cell phone? You can have the phone if you're walkin' to school with Inessa, or you can ride your bike but with no phone to tempt you. Just now I don't trust you to be careful in traffic with textin' at your fingertips."

"I'll never do something like that again, Pop, I promise. I know it was stupid," Chelsea swore. "I'd like to ride my bike. Inessa is coming on her bike ..."

"Fine, but no phone," Pop insisted.

"Pop!" Chelsea groaned. "Okay, I'll call Inessa and tell her to leave her bike home. We're walking. She prefers walking anyway."

"Good," Pop said, handing Chelsea her phone. "Now you can report to all your friends about your exciting weekend. Don't forget that you had a bad hair day on Sunday. They'll wanna know that. Right there, you'll be the talk of the town. And then you found that lip gloss marked down at the drugstore. Headline news! And, oh, you spotted a cottontail rabbit nibbling on my poor veggies."

"Oh, Pop," Chelsea giggled.

Lorenzo Spain then walked to his pickup with Athena's iPhone. He promised to drop it off at the Edson house this morning, right away.

When Pop turned the corner and saw the Edson house, a motorcycle was in the driveway. He wondered whether those idiot parents were now riding motorcycles. He wondered whether it was Trudy, the phony high school teacher, or the husband who sold bad life insurance. Pop couldn't stand either one of them. He wished Athena was not Chelsea's best friend, but she was. He figured she was a bad influence on Chelsea. But Athena wasn't really a bad girl, just an airhead. So he couldn't force Chelsea to stop seeing her best friend.

Still, Athena was allowed to do all the risky, forbidden things Chelsea couldn't do. That bothered Lorenzo Spain. Pretty soon, Pop feared, Chelsea would feel as though she was being denied some of the privileges that Athena enjoyed. Chelsea might even become rebellious.

With the phone in hand, Pop went to the door of the Edson house and rang the bell. Then, when nobody came, he rapped hard on the door. He heard a clatter of chairs.

Athena came to the door. "Oh, hi, Mr. Spain. Did you bring my phone? I missed it so much."

"Yeah, got it right here," Pop replied, looking beyond Athena to a young man sprawled on the couch. Athena was standing in the middle of the doorway. She seemed eager to take her phone, quickly close the door, and get Mr. Spain on his way. Athena didn't invite Pop into the house, but he pushed in past her. He looked at the young man and said, "Hey there, young fella."

The young man looked nervous. He had an orange lipstick smear on his cheek. Pop glanced at Athena and noticed she was wearing orange lipstick. It was that cheap kind the drugstore was selling. Chelsea had some too. Pop thought it made her look like a girl clown. "So, Athena," Pop remarked, "parents not home, eh?"

"Uh, Dad went to work. Mom is, uh, upstairs now. I think maybe she's dressing or something," Athena answered.

"Oh, good," Pop said. "I'd like to hand the phone to her like I promised. So I'll just wait for her to come down."

"I'll take it, Mr. Spain," Athena said. "Mom, uh, takes forever to dress. Come to think of it, she's probably showering, yeah."

"Funny, I don't hear no water runnin'," Pop remarked with a big grin. "In our house, you always hear that sound." The young man was about to get up, looking eagerly at the door. Pop walked over and sat beside him on the couch. "So, what'd you say your name was, dude?" Pop asked.

"I'm, uh, Athena's cousin," the boy stammered.

"Oh yeah?" Pop responded. "I guess you could say 'kissin' cousins,' right? I can see some of her orangey lipstick on your face there. All the little girls bought it on sale at the drugstore, and it just don't stay on the lips. You get what you pay for, ain't it the truth?"

He turned to Athena. "So this is your cousin, hey?"

"Yes," Athena asserted.

"I gotta go now, Athena," the boy announced, starting to get up. He looked about sixteen, maybe older. He needed a shave.

"Look, son," Pop snarled. "Y'ain't foolin' me. Y'ain't no cousin to this here little girl. An' I know what you two been doin'."

The boy exchanged a frightened look with Athena. Athena took a deep breath and confessed, "Mr. Spain, we weren't doing anything bad, I swear. Vic and I met last night at the twenty-four-seven store. We had a soda, and he said he'd come over this morning and show me some stuff on the computer. He's real good on the computer."

"Yeah, that's right," the boy gasped. "I'm a computer whiz."

"Oh, I bet you are," Pop snapped. "I bet you're a whiz in a lotta ways. So, Athena, Mom is not upstairs showering away, eh?"

"I want my iPhone," Athena whined.

"Okay," Pop announced, "here's somethin' else I know. Mama ain't upstairs. She ain't home at all."

Pop pulled out the phone. Athena's parents' business numbers were on it. Pop punched in Mr. Edson's number. He was transferred to voice mail. "Hey, Mr. Edson, Lorenzo Spain here. Lissen, I promised your wife I'd return your kid's iPhone this morning, but somethin' important come up. So why don't you or your wife stop at my house this evening after six to pick it up. You have a nice day."

The boy made a run for the door. He was outside and on his motorcycle in a few seconds.

"You can't keep my phone," Athena cried. "It's mine. That's stealing, Mr. Spain."

Pop smiled. "Hey, little girl, why don't you call the cops before you take off for school? Just tell them to come to Spain's Auto Care. That's where I'm gonna be all day." With that, Pop left the Edson house.

CHAPTER TEN

When Athena got to school, she looked for Chelsea. "Chel!" she cried when she found her walking toward science. "Your father came to my house this morning and went crazy! He wouldn't give me back my phone, and he's gonna make trouble for me!"

"What happened?" Chelsea gasped. Pop seemed quite normal at breakfast this morning.

"Oh, he came to bring the phone," Athena explained, "but my parents were gone, and he pushed his way in. Chelsea, it was awful. I had a friend over, and your father just freaked. I mean, we weren't doing anything wrong. He got so mad, he wouldn't give me back my phone. Now he's making my parents come to your house to get my phone, and I *know* he's gonna make trouble for me." Athena was crying.

"A friend?" Chelsea asked. "Not a guy!"

"Some nice kid I met at the twenty-four-seven store last night," Athena protested. "We were just talking and your father went ballistic."

Chelsea stared at Athena. She knew that look on Athena's face when she was telling only part of a story. Chelsea feared the worst was yet to come. "What else happened, Athena?"

"Poor Vic had this stupid orangey blotch on his face," Athena admitted. "You know, from that stupid lipstick we got on sale at the drugstore. I mean, I sorta kissed him *just once*. I swear it was just one quick kiss, and the dummy didn't wipe off the lipstick good enough."

"Who's the guy?" Chelsea asked, wide-eyed.

"Vic Stevens. He's a junior here," Athena told her. "Oh, Chelsea, he got so scared he just ran outta there. Chel, you gotta talk to your father so he doesn't tell my parents a lot of horrible stuff and make trouble for me."

That evening, Trudy Edson appeared at the Spain house at six thirty. Pop was sitting in the living room waiting for her. He came to the door and smiled. "Well, good evening to you, Mrs. Edson," Pop oozed. "Nice evening, ain't it? Big moon hangin' up there in the sky. Cool breeze. Couldn't ask for a nicer evening."

"Mr. Spain," Trudy Edson said in an annoyed voice, "I have tons of homework for my classes, and I have to create lesson plans. This is quite an inconvenience to have to come over here to get our daughter's iPhone."

"Oh, hey, I'm sorry, Mrs. Edson," Pop responded. "I just wanted a few words with you, dear lady. I know you're one of those busy professionals who got no time for their own kids. Believe me, I appreciate that. But this morning when I went to your home to return the iPhone, there was nobody there but little fourteen-year-old Athena. Oh, and this pimply faced bearded young kid, name of Vic Stevens. He was loungin' on the couch with orange lipstick all over his face. Naturally, I felt compelled to let you know that a kissin' party was goin' on over there after you guys hurried off to your important jobs."

"*What?*" Trudy Edson gasped.

"Oh yeah!" Pop asserted. "You know my Chelsea and your Athena bought this cut-rate orangey lipstick at the drugstore, and it don't stay on the lips. This guy, he had it all over his cheek. It was smeared on Athena's lips too, like she'd been busy as a little kissin' bee. Didn't look so good, Trudy. May I call you Trudy? You can call me Lorenzo if you want to."

"*Mr.* Spain," Mrs. Edson answered sharply, "Athena may have given this boy a quick kiss when he stopped to drop off a book or something. But nothing nasty was going on, as you are implying. I happen to trust my daughter. Now if I may have our iPhone, I must get back to my work."

"Oh yeah," Pop handed her the iPhone. "And one more thing, my daughter ain't never coming to your house again. Y'hear me?"

Mom was in the hallway listening. Jaris and Chelsea were with her.

"And if Athena comes here, we're gonna be keeping an eye on her," Pop advised. "In this house, no sixteen-year-old bearded punks play kissin' games with fourteen-year-old girls. You got a lot to learn about being a mother, lady. You maybe know all there is in the world about teaching high school. But you ain't got a clue about bein' a mother."

"You are a very rude man, Mr. Spain," Mrs. Edson stated, turning on her very high heels and stomping out of the house.

"Wow!" Mom exclaimed, emerging from the darkness of the hall.

"Good for you, Pop," Jaris said.

"Athena will never speak to me again," Chelsea murmured.

"If that's the truth," Pop told his daughter, "which I very much fear it ain't, this is your lucky day, little girl."

In the weeks ahead, the Tubman freshman boys and girls involved in the play *Courage* spent many days rehearsing for it. Chelsea and Heston had the biggest parts, so they were the most deeply involved. But everybody was working hard, including Athena. She had a minor role as one of the house slaves, who sometimes worked alongside Harriet Tubman shucking corn. Right after the incident with the iPhone, Chelsea feared Athena was seriously mad at her. After all, Pop had insulted Athena's mother that night. But Athena did not seem to be angry at all.

One day, as two girls walked home from school, Athena made a comment. "I never met anyone like your father, Chelsea."

Chelsea shrugged. "I guess not," she admitted. Chelsea wasn't sure what Athena meant. Lorenzo Spain was the only father Chelsea ever knew. Although she often thought he was a little over-the-top, she loved him with all her heart. She felt loved by him too.

Chelsea felt safe because of her father. She had many friends with fathers who were there for them most or at least some of the time. Pop was there all the time. He never pushed Chelsea or Jaris into sports. He never pushed them into anything. He was just there—big and strong and always there. Chelsea never doubted that, whatever happened, he would be behind her. When she was small, she thought that God must be a little like Lorenzo Spain. As she grew older, Chelsea saw Pop's flaws. But she never doubted that he would give up his life in a minute for her or Jaris or Mom. Nothing mattered to him more than his family.

"My father is much different than yours, Chelsea," Athena said.

"I guess all fathers are a little different," Chelsea commented.

"He laughed," Athena said.

"Who laughed?" Chelsea asked.

"My father," Athena answered, "when he found out Vic was there with me. He just laughed. He didn't come down on me or anything. He said your pop is a throwback to olden times. Nowadays, fathers let their kids do their thing. They think it's okay to let us be free, you know. My dad says if I want to hang at the twenty-four-seven store, I should be careful, but it's okay. He trusts me."

"I can't imagine doing that," Chelsea admitted.

"I get to do a lot of stuff you can't do, Chel," Athena said.

"I guess you're lucky in a way," Chelsea told her.

"Yeah. Your father's like a big, old wild bear fighting for his cubs. Like the world is a dark and dangerous place. It's like he's gotta watch out for you all the time," Athena suggested.

"I guess," Chelsea agreed.

"He loves you a lot," Athena said.

"Your father loves you too, Athena," Chelsea told her friend.

Athena looked at Chelsea and smiled, but she didn't say anything before running off.

When Chelsea got in the house, her father was just coming home too. He was still greasy and dirty from the garage. He hadn't changed and showered yet.

Chelsea ran to Pop and gave him a big hug.

"Hey, hey, hey, little girl, what's this about?" Pop asked, laughing.

"I just felt like it," Chelsea told him before going to her room to read her lines one more time.

The presentation of *Courage* took place at Tubman High on a Friday night. The Spain family left early, as Chelsea was stricken with last-minute jitters. She had done well in the dress rehearsal. But she worried that, at the last minute, she'd forget everything. As her family took their places in the front row, Chelsea hurried onstage to join the cast.

Heston looked terrific in his torn white shirt. He grinned at Chelsea, and they fist-bumped. Chelsea peeked through the curtains at the audience in the auditorium, which was rapidly filling up. Mom, Pop, Jaris, and all their friends were there. Mickey Jenkins had come with her son Trevor. She rarely came to anything, but here she was. Kevin Walker was there with his grandparents.

Chelsea kept telling herself she would do all right, but she couldn't shake her nerves completely.

Suddenly someone not in the cast appeared backstage.

"Grandma Jessie!" Chelsea gasped. Her beautiful silver-haired grandmother was standing there, holding a lovely pale blue dress with little velvet collar and cuffs.

"Sweetheart," Grandma Jessie said, "you are such a lovely girl. It's a shame you have to wear those shabby old dresses

188

on stage. I'm sure little Harriet Tubman had one pretty dress laid aside that she could wear for special occasions. So perhaps in one scene you might—"

Mr. Wingate came running with Jeannie Duvall on his heels. "No, no, *no*, dear lady," Mr. Wingate gasped. "Chelsea is perfectly costumed for the part."

"She's my granddaughter," Grandma Jessie insisted. "I just thought for one little scene, she might wear this," Grandma Jessie waved the lovely garment in the air. "Oh … and must she be *barefoot* too?"

"Come, my dear," Mr. Wingate said to Grandma Jessie, gently taking her arm and leading her offstage out the back way. "I'm sure you will enjoy your granddaughter's performance." He led her to her seat beside Monica Spain.

"Oh, Mom," Monica Spain groaned.

"I tried to bring her a prettier dress," Grandma Jessie explained. "You should see how she looks back there. The poor child is dressed in a hideous gray thing. And she's *barefoot*."

Chelsea peeked from the curtains again. She saw Pop laughing. He was laughing so hard, he was shaking. Somehow, Grandma Jessie's unexpected appearance backstage dissolved all Chelsea's fears. She laughed too, and she joined the cast as the curtain rose.

First came the sweet, sad strains of "Go Down, Moses," the old slave hymn. Then Chelsea Spain and the others playing the slaves began going through the motions of shucking corn. As Harriet, Chelsea suddenly straightened and stared up at the evening star painted on the scenery. Her face showed the hope and courage of fifteen-year-old Harriet as she first dreamed of freedom from her grim life. In a few more years, she would make her break for freedom. Then she would lead many more over the same path.

In a big dramatic moment, Heston Crawford, as the slave boy, broke for freedom. Chelsea stared after him with love and hope. An overseer appeared, shouting for him to stop. Chelsea, as Harriet, blocked the overseer from pursuing the boy, and he fled. The overseer hurled the lead that struck the girl in the head. She fell and lay motionless on the stage. Then, slowly she rose, injured, dazed, but not defeated. She stumbled and rose again, stumbled and crawled on, holding her wounded head.

The audience broke into cheers. They cheered for the bravery of the woman they were honoring tonight, the namesake of their high school. But they also cheered for the girl who played Harriet with such conviction and heart.

At the end of the performance, Chelsea and the other cast members held hands and took a bow. Jeannie Duvall presented Chelsea with a bouquet of roses and whispered, "Darling, you were magnificent."

But Chelsea saw just one thing: Mom, Pop, Jaris, and Grandma Jessie, united as they rarely were, on their feet, clapping and cheering.

Jaris caught sight of Trevor Jenkins walking from the school auditorium alone. His mother had to go to work at the nursing home. A friend was driving her away. Trevor looked down in the dumps, and Jaris knew exactly why: Amberlynn.

Jaris walked over to Trevor and put his hands on his friend's shoulders. "Bro, your girl's out there, and you'll find her," Jaris assured him.

Trevor turned with a limp smile.

"You'll find your chick, dude. I promise you," Jaris asserted. "She'll be there, and she'll be everything you always hoped for and more. Trust me."

"You think?" Trevor asked.

"*I know*," Jaris affirmed. "Where you going now?"

"Home, I guess," Trevor responded. "Ma hadda go to work."

"Pop's making hamburgers at home, even bigger and sloppier than we had at George's," Jaris told him. "Come on."

"No, man, it's a *family* celebration," Trevor objected.

"And you're family, dude. You're my bro'," Jaris told his best friend. Grinning, Jaris threw his arm around Trevor as they walked to the Spain car.

As they walked, Trevor was still thinking about Amberlynn. He had wanted to make her his girlfriend, and he still wanted that. He could not get her beautiful face out of his head. He saw her there, smiling at him.

"I'd make you happy in every way I could, every day," he vowed to her, in his mind. "I'd do anything for you … if you were mine."

Jaris was also lost in thought. But his thoughts were about hamburgers—Pop's big, hot, juicy hamburgers.